THE CEMETERY OF EUROPE

BY THE SAME AUTHOR

The Cemetery of Europe

The Spanish Play
The German Connection
The Murphy Girls

three plays by
Seamus Finnegan

Marion Boyars
London · New York

Published in Great Britian and the United States in 1991
by Marion Boyars Publishers
24 Lacy Road, London SW15 1NL
26 East 33rd Street, New York, NY 10016

Distributed in the United States and Canada by
Rizzoli International Publications, New York

Distributed in Australia by
Wild & Woolley, Glebe, N.S.W.

British Library Cataloguing in Publication Data
Finnegan, Seamus, *1949*–
    The cemetery of Europe; The Spanish play; The
    German connection; The Murphy girls: three plays.
    I. Finnegan, Seamus, *1949*–. Spanish play
    II. Finnegan, Seamus, *1949*–. German connection
    III. Finnegan, Seamus, *1949*–. Murphy girls
    822'.914

Library of Congress Cataloging-in-Publication Data
Finnegan, Seamus, 1949–
    The cemetery of Europe; The Spanish play; The German
    connection; The Murphy girls: three plays / by Seamus
Finnegan.
    1. World War, 1939–1945—
Drama. I. Title. II. Title: Cemetery
    of Europe.
    PR6056.I5188C4   1989
    822'.914—dc20   89–22242

ISBN 0-7145-2895-1 Original Paperback Edition

Typeset in Helvetica and 10/11½ Times
by Ann Buchan (Typesetters), Middlesex

Printed and bound in Great Britain by
Southampton Book Company

CONTENTS

ACKNOWLEDGEMENTS

Julia Pascal
Marion Boyars & Staff
Patricia MacNaughton
Mike Dowling & his family
Michael Longley & Northern Ireland Arts Council
Camden Arts
Greater London Arts
The sadly missed GLC
Kathryn Baird of the BBC
Ned Chaillet of the BBC
and all others associated with
or who helped in the production
of these three plays

**IN MEMORY OF MY MOTHER &
FOR MY FATHER**

THE CEMETERY OF EUROPE
An Introduction

The Spanish Play is the story of two working class Irishmen,
one Catholic, one Protestant, who unite with others from
different countries, religions and classes to fight for the
humanitarian ideals of freedom and socialism. They are
defeated as was the Spanish Republic by the forces of
fascism with the aid and connivance of Western 'democra-
cies' and the Catholic Church:

> And you wanna know, Father, what the forces of
> Christianity did then, not simply satisfied with killing
> all and everyone — they stuck little pictures, little
> 'holy' pictures in the dead bodies. 'Holy' pictures that
> showed a bleeding Sacred Heart and General Franco
> hand in bloody hand. That's what I saw, Father
> O'Neill.

They witnessed priests, bishops, cardinals and nuns give the
falangist salute. Today, in parts of Europe, we witness the
demise of 'Socialism'. We witness the downfall of 'totalita-
rian' states. The West dances and applauds the disintegra-
tion of the Red Empire, but what else do we perceive? We
also see, if we look closely enough, priests, bishops and
cardinals crawling out from underneath their clerical stones,
ready and willing to impose their own ideological straitjack-
ets in Poland, Czechoslovakia and Hungary. Are these
people the mentors and agents of freedom and democracy?

We hear a Polish Pope proclaim 'the spiritual unity of Christian Europe'.

Is this the same European Christian 'spiritual unity' that just fifty years ago was responsible for the Shoah of six million Jews?

Is this the same Catholic Church that only recently 'forgave' the Jews the death of Jesus?

Is this the same Catholic Church that has yet to face up to its complicity in that crime of crimes, the Holocaust?

Is this the same Pope who goes to GERMANY to canonize a Jewish martyr, Edith Stein?

Is this Pope the same leader of freedom who allows a Carmellite convent to exist in the death camp of Auschwitz?

I was born and brought up in Ireland, a country where the majority are Catholic and where the Catholic Church has never helped the people in their fight against oppression. Indeed it is a country where the Catholic church has always connived, and still connives, with the Government and forces of repression. And yet the majority of people still flock to its altars. Is this all down to fear? Fear and terror of a religion and Church that promises damnation if its 'faithful' don't kowtow to the dictates of the men in Roman robes? The Catholic Church in Ireland has invaded the minds of the people and systematically murdered any attempts at free thought. Religions, like many ideologies, are concerned with achieving and holding power. They do not take kindly to the notions of freedom and liberty. They rule by fear; and fear of a thought system will always be greater than the fear of tanks and guns. Some people in Ireland may attack an occupying army but they have yet to attack or acknowledge the Roman Catholic power that occupies their minds. Those in other parts of Europe would do well to watch their backs. Totalitarianism moves in many mysterious ways.

The German Connection is the story of a working class Irishman who rejects the narrow confines of his nationalist forefathers, fights the forces of Nazism and dies to free Europe.

Today, in parts of Europe, we witness the clamour and din of tribal allegiances as they parade and wave their flags and emblems. 'This bit of earth belongs to the X people.' 'We are the Y's.' 'The Z's demand secession and their own nation state.'

In Ireland, I was suckled at the teats of nationalism. For the last twenty years I have observed nationalism and tribal identities murder and torture each other on these two Western isles of Britain and Ireland. For the last ten years I have written over a dozen plays trying, as poet Seamus Heaney puts it, 'to set the darkness echoing'. Conclusion? There are no conclusions. But what I believe most passionately is that anything that turns people inward and apart results in killing and dying before one's time, while that which draws us out and toward each other might, just might, lead to enlightenment and a longer life.

The Murphy Girls is the story of a working class Irish woman in exile. Alienated from her own, alien to her hosts, she knows not where she belongs. She has escaped the nets of nationality and religion but is caught in the web of self-doubt. Perhaps, the only true home for us all is the grave.

I live in a city called London. In that city lives a writer. A writer condemned to death by the high priests of a religion that is fearful of rebellious words. A writer who for more than a year now has been in hiding. A writer who, like all good writers, has challenged the orthodoxy of his background. In a part of Eastern Europe, the playwright Vaclav Havel has been elected President of his country. In a part of Western Europe, Salman Rushdie remains a condemned man. This introduction is dedicated to him. Let freedom reach him soon.

Seamus Finnegan
Autumn 1990

THE SPANISH PLAY

**A play
in 16 scenes**

THE SPANISH PLAY was first performed in 1986 at the
Place Theatre, London.

CAST

BILLY ROBINSON	Mike Dowling
JIMMY ROBINSON	Toby Byrne
ROSIE ROBINSON	Annie Raitt
FATHER O'NEILL	Jim Millea
TOMMY REID	Michael McKnight
SAMMY COHEN	Steve Simmonds
FELICITY SMYTHE	Sarah Martin
MARIA	Norma Cohen
CATALONIAN PEASANT	Mercedes Dalmases

Other parts played by the cast and members of the
London Contemporary School of Dance.
The play was directed by Julia Pascal.

CHARACTERS

BILLY ROBINSON
JIMMY ROBINSON
ROSIE ROBINSON
FATHER O'NEILL
TOMMY REID
SAMMY COHEN
FELICITY SMYTHE
MARIA
CATALONIAN PEASANT (OLD WOMAN)
A MAN
JOHN CORNWALL
JEANNE
A GUIDE
FATHER CUNNINGHAM
GENERAL GAVAN O'DUFFY
A LORD MAYOR
A MONSIGNOR
TWO GESTAPO OFFICERS
FATHER GAMBARA

SCENE 1

Belfast. The home of the Robinson family, working class Catholics.

BILLY: I've made up my mind. I'm going. I leave for Spain on Monday. I packed up the job the night. Asked for my cards — the lot.

JIMMY: You what? You packed up your job? What sort of a bloody eejit are you, Billy? Jobs aren't that easy to come by in this city, you know, even for a good bricklayer. And I'll grant you, you have a quare pair of hands when it comes to building brick. But Jesus, you've obviously got cement in that head of yours. Spain? What the hell are you going to Spain for?

BILLY: To fight, Da. Their fight is our fight. The people of Spain, the working class. . .

JIMMY: To fight? To fight? Well, if you wanna fight, there's plenty of fightin' to be done in Ireland. What about 'the people' of Ireland? What about the 'working class' here? What about the working class in your own city? There's plenty of fighting needs to be done here without going over to some bloody foreign land to join forces with a load of bloody Communists and Bolshemicks. Have you read, son, what those wonderful people of Spain are actually doing? Pillaging churches. Shooting priests. Raping nuns. And bombing children in their Catholic schools.

BILLY: Propaganda, Da. Reactionary propaganda. It's the old story, that. Where are such stories coming from? They're not coming from the friends of the working class in

Ireland. Christ, you should know that. You of all people. Those lies and distortions are coming from the same mouths, from those same people who decried and condemned the likes of you in 1916. Jesus, Da, you were one of Pearse's volunteers; can you not see the connection?

JIMMY: No, Billy, I cannot. There isn't one. We were fighting for national freedom. . .

BILLY: And what the hell do you think the Spanish people are fighting for? They're fighting in defence of their Republic. A duly elected democratic republic, Da. It's a bunch of Fascists that have plotted against them. Landowners and conservative churchmen, the same cowboys that spat on the likes of you in your fight for freedom.

JIMMY: Aye, Billy, our fight was for freedom. But our freedom fight didn't entail shooting down the Catholic clergy. Our fight wasn't a fight for atheism. Communism! Our fight for freedom was a fight to be allowed to be Catholics. To have a clergy that wasn't hounded and hunted. And it's a fight that still goes on today in this very city of ours, Billy. Or have you forgotten about the recent riots and 'pogroms' against Catholics. Have you forgotten that we Catholics in Ireland have suffered persecution and oppression for our faith. Have you forgotten the penal days in Ireland, Billy? For the way you're talking would seem to me that you have, so bloody keen are you to leave your own country and people.

BILLY: No, Father, I haven't forgotten any of those things. And I'm not arguing with you about them.

JIMMY: Well, what the hell are you arguing about then, Billy? About going to fight somewhere that you know nothing about? About going to fight in a foreigner's war that has nothing to do with us?

BILLY: But it has, Da. It has to do with us. It's the same bloody war, the same fight, the same struggle — can't you see? Jesus, how can I make you understand? Ma, you understand, don't you? You know what I'm talking about?

JIMMY: Never mind bringing your Ma into this, Billy. Politics is not wimmin's business.

ROSIE: Oh is it not, Jimmy Robinson? Well, I have news for you. It is as much my business as it is the likes of yours.

JIMMY: Rosie. . .

ROSIE: Don't you Rosie me, Jimmy Robinson. For I know all there is to know about politics. You don't have to be a man in a uniform marching up and down with a hurley stick on your shoulder to know about war. Let me remind you, Jimmy, that my young brother died in my arms. Aye, in these same very arms that have held you in bed of a night, and cradled you, Billy, from when you were born — these arms held our Bobby's riddled body when he was shot by the Black and Tans during the War of Independence. These arms nursed his dying breath on that doorstep out there. Remember, Jimmy. And the life flowing fast from him, cut down as he was coming home from his work by those who were denying us any existence never mind 'freedom'. Don't you kid yourself, Patrick Pearse, Rosie and women know too well about the fight for this freedom and that freedom. And if our Billy stands there now and honestly tells me, his mother, that he must go to Spain to fight, for their fight is our fight, then I will weep for him, but I will not stand in his way. Don't go, I would plead with you, Billy, but for reasons other than those of your father. But if you do still go, let it not be long before you return safely to your mother's arms.

Billy and his mother embrace.
Jimmy looks on.

ROSIE: Maybe by the time you return, Billy, son, your Da'll have changed his views on politics. And women.

Billy and his mother laugh.
Jimmy angrily knocks out his pipe muttering to himself.

2 | SCENE

Sound of Big Ben.
A house in Litchfield Street, London.

MAN: You realize, Comrade, that what you are embarking on is illegal since the enactment of the Non-Intervention Agreement.

BILLY: I do, Comrade.

MAN: Yes, the Mother of Parliaments and of so-called democracy, by standing aside like Pontius Pilate, tacitly gives support to the Fascists these days. But she will rue the day that she embraced such cowardice, for if we lose, she will be next in line for attack. Spain's fight is our fight, and if my country, if England, now stands aside from the battle with evil it will not be long before that evil turns its attention beyond the borders of Spain. The signs are there throughout Europe, Comrade.

BILLY: They've already been visiting us in Ireland.

MAN: Yes. We've been observing closely the antics of General Gavan O'Duffy and his Blueshirts.

BILLY: He and his kind are a slur on the name of Ireland, Comrade. The Irish, more than anyone else, should know better.

MAN: But, unfortunately, Comrade, it is often those who should know better who cause *us* the greater headache.

BILLY: But O'Duffy and his Blueshirts are not representative of Ireland, Comrade. They have no right to the nationality of Ireland. None at all.

MAN: Please, Comrade. I wasn't implying. . .

BILLY: I know you weren't, Comrade. It's just it makes me angry that anyone should shame the name of Ireland in such a way. And (*Billy smiles*) to have it mentioned by an Englishman makes the blood boil against them even more.

MAN: I understand that, Comrade Robinson. But our fight, the reason we are here, the reason *you* are here, is proof that national boundaries are *not* what we are primarily concerned with. Now, to get back to why you are here. These are your tickets and documents. You will be travelling overnight by way of the Newhaven-Dieppe steamer. Then by train to Paris. Upon your arrival in Paris, you will make your way to this hotel on the Left Bank. (*shows card*) You've memorized the name of the hotel?

BILLY: Yes, Comrade.

MAN: There, at the hotel, you will be contacted and taken to another of our assembly points in Paris for further briefing and medical examination. Two points. One, at this briefing you will be given a kind of 'political examination' — there is no other term for it. You are not to take offence at this. It is not meant to denigrate your integrity but we have found it to be a necessary, if inconvenient precaution. It ensures we do not involve adventurers.

BILLY: I understand, Comrade.

MAN: The second point is this. If you are challenged by the French police on your journey or while you are still in Paris, you are 'weekending', a short weekend holiday of the sort popular with the upper classes is what you are indulging yourself in.

BILLY: I get the picture, Comrade.

MAN: And finally, Comrade Robinson, if anything should happen that isn't meant to, we are unable to help. In fact, we know nothing of your existence at all. Is that clear?

BILLY: Yes.

Enter Tommy Reid.
Man turns to Tommy.

MAN: Come in, Comrade. Let me introduce you to your fellow weekender. Comrade Robinson, this is Comrade Reid.

BILLY: Billy Robinson, Comrade. (*They shake hands*)

TOMMY: Tommy Reid. Pleased to meet you.

BILLY: You're not from Belfast. . .?

MAN: A small world, is it not, Comrades? Especially, as you would say, you both kick with the wrong foot.

Exit man.

BILLY: How did he, an Englishman, know about 'kicking with the wrong foot'?

TOMMY: Oh, I've been filling him in on our local politics. He mentioned to me that my fellow weekender was a Taig!

BILLY: Christ, I don't believe this. Where are you from, Tommy?

TOMMY: (*Mock solemn*) Belfast! (*Tommy laughs*)

BILLY: I know that.

TOMMY: (*Laughing*) Shankill Road. You?

BILLY: (*Laughing*) Falls!

TOMMY: Jesus, we're landed, aren't we?

BILLY: Christ, you can say that again. A Taig and a Prod, Comrades, on their way to Spain together!

TOMMY: So here tell us, how did a Mick like you get a name like Billy, for Christ's sake? Did somebody turn?

BILLY: Aye. My grandfather. He was from the Shankill, would you believe?

TOMMY: I believe. And don't tell me. He married your grandmother who was a Catholic and then sold his Grand Protestant Orange heritage down the papish aisle so that all the wee Robinsons like your Da, could be reared good papes.

BILLY: There you have it.

TOMMY: I knew it.

BILLY: But here, Tommy, *Reid*'s not exactly a Protestant name. Did some of our lot take the soup?

TOMMY: If they were anything to do with our family they took whatever they could get their hands on, bones and all. Jesus, I can hear them at home — so, how'd you get on in the International Brigade, Tommy? Did you meet any 'foreigners'? Aye. My comrade weekender was a Taig from the Falls!

BILLY: That's foreign enough to them!

SCENE | 3

Music: 'The Internationale' sung in French.
Paris.
A hotel room.
Sammy Cohen, John Cornwall and Felicity Smythe in conversation.
Enter Billy and Tommy.

SAMMY: Welcome, Comrades. Sammy Cohen's the name.

BILLY: Billy Robinson. Pleased to meet you, Sammy.

TOMMY: Tommy Reid. Good to see you, Comrade.

SAMMY: And this here is Felicity Smythe.

FELICITY: Billy. (*Shakes hands*) Tommy. (*Shakes hands. And they look at each other for that extra moment*)

SAMMY: And John Cornwall.

BILLY: John.

JOHN: How do you do?

BILLY: And this is — Tommy!

TOMMY: Yes. Yes. I'm here. Hello John. (*Shakes hands*)

Tommy looks back at Felcity who smiles.
Enter French comrade, Jeanne.

JEANNE: Comrades. Attention for a moment *s'il vous plaît*. I will try to speak English. But for me it is not easy. *Parlez-vous français*, anyone?

JOHN: *Oui.*

FELICITY: *Un peu.*

BILLY/TOMMY/SAMMY: *Non!*

Everyone laughs.

JEANNE: *Ça va très bien.* The accent is perfect.

TOMMY: *Merci beaucoup, Mademoiselle.*

More laughter.

JEANNE: Comrades. Thank you for bearing with us on the political examinations. A necessity, I am afraid. But it is good to know you are all so healthy. Just a few words, *s'il vous plaît*. I cannot warn you enough of the dangers you will face in Spain. It is not a pleasant task ahead of you. The battle conditions are unequal. *Très* unequal. The Fascists are growing stronger and stronger. They have the arms and the ammunition. As you know, they have the support of the Fascists of Germany and Italy. Those who pretend to be our allies refuse to help us. The Republic, the people of Spain are alone. Except — except for you, their international comrades who are selflessly prepared to fight. For you know that the war of Spain is the war of all of us who believe in freedom. But, Comrades, freedom can demand sacrifices of us and, without being too gloomy about it, some of you may make the supreme sacrifice. I say this only to impress upon you the seriousness of the situation and to offer a last opportunity to anyone who even now may wish to withdraw. Please — for it is not only your own life that will be in danger but those of your comrades — withdraw now, there is still time, if you have any doubts at all.

Long pause.
No one moves. All eyes on Jeanne.
Merci beaucoup, Comrades. And now to practical matters. Tomorrow morning, you will travel by rail to Beziers, a small town in the south of France. You will travel in small groups of two or three. Each group will not indicate that it knows any other group. But you will all be

watching a man, a comrade, who will be sitting alone. You will not communicate with that comrade but when he leaves the train at Beziers, you will follow him discreetly in your separate groups. Taxis will be waiting for you at the station to drive you to your hotel. There you will stay and wait. One day. Maybe two. You will not on any account leave your hotel or venture into the town. A French comrade will then collect you and drive you to our concentration point. You will wait there until nightfall. Then you will be taken by bus to the foot of the Pyrenees for the last stage of your journey to war. (*Pause*) One last important piece of advice, Comrades. Bring plenty of tobacco with you!

Laughter.

JEANNE: Good luck, Comrades. And *au revoir.*

Light change, during which set up props for next scene.

SCENE | 4

Silence.
A barn near the foot of the Pyrenees.

BILLY: Here, Tommy, did you hear that? This man here was at Cambridge University.

TOMMY: Who?

BILLY: John. Writes poetry as well. Has had stuff published.

TOMMY: How long have you left Cambridge, John?

JOHN: I came down six months ago.

TOMMY: Came down? Where to?

BILLY: Jesus, it's a saying, meaning you left, finished, graduated.

Pay no attention to him, John, he's a Protestant, knows nothing. His sort don't have a culture.

JOHN: But I'm a Protestant.

TOMMY: Ha! Ha! You're stymied there, clever Fenian features.

BILLY: But he's an English Protestant. They're different, you Orange eejit.

TOMMY: I think you better be careful, Billy, for I've a feeling you're in a minority of one in this company. I have a feeling you're the only Taig. Am I right, Felicity?

FELICITY: Taig? What's a Taig?

TOMMY: It's Belfast slang for Catholic. You're not a Catholic are you, Felicity?

FELICITY: No. I'm not a Catholic. The family are Church of England, but I. . .

TOMMY: See, Billy. I told you. (*To Felicity*) My mother'd love you — Church of England. Sorry, Felicity, you were saying.

FELICITY: I was just going to say I'm a member of the British Communist Party.

BILLY: (*To Tommy*) Your Ma certainly won't love her if she finds out she's a Communist. There's only one step lower down the rung than that for a born and bred Shankill Road woman. Communist! Fenian! They were all made in hell is what your Ma'll say. No, afraid not Tommy, you can't take her home to the Shankill Road.

Tommy makes a swipe at Billy. Felicity smiles.

JOHN: What about you, Sammy? Where would you fit into all this tribal allegiance?

SAMMY: Me? I'm outside the lot of you. Jew, aren't I? Cockney Jew and a Communist Jew! Parents from Russia. Well, I mean, *mates, I'm* the one with the proper credentials for round here and this job we're on, aren't I?

Laughter.
Cross-fade to Felicity standing by barn window.
Tommy follows her. Others acknowledge with nod.
Pause.

TOMMY: Do you mind if I stand here and talk to you, Felicity?

FELICITY: Of course not, Tommy. Why should I?

TOMMY: Can I ask you a question?

Pause.
Felicity turns to him.

TOMMY: Why did you join the Brigade, Felicity?

Felicity turns away to look out.
Pause.

FELICITY: I believe in the cause. Why did you?

TOMMY: Same.

Pause.
But — you're a woman.

FELICITY: And are women not allowed to believe in causes?

TOMMY: No. No. I didn't mean that. I'm sorry. I didn't mean to give any offence. Maybe I should go back. . .

FELICITY: No. Don't go.

They stand looking out.
I'm a painter, Tommy. Least that's that I did in London before I joined the Brigade.

TOMMY: Pictures, you mean.

FELICITY: Yes. Landscapes mostly. Some portraits of friends, family.

TOMMY: The only painters I've met were house-painters on building sites.

Pause.

FELICITY: Why do you do that?

TOMMY: Do what?

FELICITY: Put yourself down. I've noticed that about most Irish people I've met. Everything's a joke. Even when they're talented and recognized as such — writers, painters. . .

TOMMY: Do they? Maybe it's survival. And Irish people don't like anyone with airs and graces, even if they're talented.

FELICITY: Do you think I have airs and graces, Tommy?

TOMMY: No. But you have to remember, Felicity, anyone who talks like you to an Irish person, they're — a bit — grand. It's our training, if you like. Posh English accents to us, even Protestant Irishmen, means oppression.

FELICITY: I understand that. But I can't help the way I speak. I was born to that but I wasn't born to be here. To be waiting in a barn with four strange men, waiting to go to war. I wasn't born to be a painter either. My family and friends don't take it seriously. They see it as a pretty hobby. Dabbling in watercolours, my mother calls it. And it puts men off, she says. They feel threatened.

TOMMY: Do they?

They smile.

FELICITY: Yes. My mother is right — prospective English middle-class husbands don't want anything but the full and complete attention of their wives. But that's not what I'm talking about.

TOMMY: I'm enjoying listening anyhow.

FELICITY: You asked me a question, Tommy. Why am I here?

TOMMY: You don't have to answer. I didn't want to start anything.

FELICITY: But it's a question I keep asking myself. And I must keep asking it of myself. You see, Tommy, I nearly turned back when we were in Paris. You remember when the French comrade asked if anyone wished to withdraw. I nearly stepped forward. Not because of the war. Not because of the horror and danger she talked about. I am afraid. I am very frightened, don't misunderstand me — but I was more afraid that I was one of those 'adventurers'. I kept asking myself was I just here for personal reasons? Was I just going to Spain to spite my mother, my family, my friends? It's not the done thing this, you know, for an upper middle-class English girl whose father works in Whitehall. . .

TOMMY: Please, Felicity. You don't have to explain.

FELICITY: But I must. I must to myself. You see, in a way I believe it's no different from painting pictures and being scorned. I had to fight for the freedom to do that. So, it's only a further step to fight for a greater freedom for others. (*Pause*) Isn't it?

Tommy nods.

TOMMY: It's a great thing you are doing.

FELICITY: It's a selfish thing, Tommy. You see, there's no point in trying to paint beautiful pictures if there's no one free to look at them.

Hold on Felicity and Tommy.
Cross-fade back to Billy, John and Sammy.

BILLY: Do you think we'll be moving soon, Comrades?

JOHN: It can't be much longer. It's been dark for ages now. Let's hope nothing has happened to our guides.

SAMMY: Be right up the creek, mates, if anything has. What'll we do if they don't show, eh?

JOHN: Please, Sammy. It doesn't bear thinking about. I wish they'd get a move on otherwise they'll find five frozen volunteers. I didn't realize it got as cold as this in Europe at night.

Silence.
Sammy laughs.

BILLY: What's so funny, Sammy?

Sammy laughs again.

BILLY: Well? What is it?

SAMMY: Nothing really. But it's funny the things come into your mind at times. I was just listening to you both talking about the guides and that and wondering when they'll come — when into my mind came a picture — a picture of what I suppose were my ancestors — only they looked like us. It was like we were all Jews — you boys as well as me. And Tommy and Felicity. Jews. Waiting for guides. Waiting for somebody to come to take them from the village before the Cossacks arrived — before the next pogrom. I hadn't thought about it before, but I suppose this is a bit like what it was like for them. Always travelling. Running from place to place. Holed up one place, then another. Always on the move. Waiting. Huddled together. Not knowing what was going to happen to them. Or where they were going. Moving on. Waiting. Running. Cold, frightened, terrified. Only difference being we've chosen this. They didn't have a choice. Did they?

Enter Tommy and Felicity.

TOMMY: They're here.

BILLY: The guides?

SAMMY: The Messiah?

TOMMY: No. The bloody Orange Order!

FELICITY: Yes. The guides.

JOHN: At last.

Enter guide.

GUIDE: *!Salud, compañeros!*

ALL: *!Salud!*

Light change, abstract music.
All in formation, spots on each. Trudging over bridge.

FELICITY: Through the darkness, figures appear. Our guides, in rope sandals known as alparagats. Shoes exchanged for these alparagats. Then with a gesture from the guide we follow through a field. No smoking. No lights. No talking. They are watching for us. If we obey orders we *will* get through. The border is at the top of the mountain. It will take us all night to get there. It will be rough but we *will* make it, *compañeros*.

BILLY: We climb over rocks, boulders, dry creeks and gullies. The path leads up and up and up. We fall. We ache. We fall again. And again.

GUIDE: *Allez, camarades! Allez!*

JOHN: I dislodge a pebble but hear no sound of its fall. We are on the edge of a precipice.

GUIDE: Stay on the path, or you will be killed.

TOMMY: The hours pass. And more hours. I feel tired. Sore. The air is cold but it is also sweet. I can see lights. Like fairy lights on a Christmas tree. Winking. Beckoning. Winking.

GUIDE: *Voilà, la frontière d'Espagne!*

SAMMY: The sun is rising. Slowly. Majestically. We stand as one. Tired and with aching eyes, we gaze upon the land of Iberia.

FELCITY: Gone are the doubts. The cold. The pain. The misery. Gone is the past. It is good to be alive under this morning

Spanish sun. We are young. We have arrived in the future!

All sing 'The Internationale'.

SCENE | 5

Single church bell. Belfast. We see Rosie and Jimmy as in Scene 1. On either side of them, raised as in pulpits, are two priests, Fr. Cunningham and Fr. O'Neill. Silence.

FATHER O'NEILL: My dear people, the fight in Spain is a fight between the rich privileged classes and the poor oppressed working class. The cause being fought in Spain is closer to us than we perhaps realize. The Foreign Legion and Moroccan troops are to Spain what the Black and Tans were to Ireland. Did the Spanish people send men to join the Black and Tans? No. Did they take up collections in their churches to help the Black and Tans? No.

Cut to Father Cunningham. Father O'Neill continues to mime speech.

FATHER CUNNINGHAM: My dear people, the contest in Spain is not a struggle between political parties as to who should rule, but between God and His enemies. The account of the atrocities committed in Spain has filled the Catholic world with dismay. Many fear that the Spanish disturbance will upset the fabric of European peace. The war in Spain is between Christianity and Communism and it is through prayer — the atonement for past crimes — that we can render the greatest help to our afflicted brethren and the cause of Christian civilization.

Cut to Rosie and Jimmy.
Fathers O'Neill and Cunningham continue to mime.
Silence.

ROSIE: There was a letter from our Billy the day, Jimmy.

Pause.

ROSIE: Oi, Jimmy! Are you tea leaf or what?

JIMMY: Eh? What's that Rosie? What are you saying, woman? Can a man not get peace to read the daily newspaper?

ROSIE: Don't you talk to me about peace, Jimmy Robinson. And don't you 'woman' me. I said, there was a letter came the day from our Billy.

JIMMY: Was there?

Pause.

ROSIE: Well?

JIMMY: Well, what for Jesus' sake?

ROSIE: Well, do you wanna read it?

Rosie holds out envelope to Jimmy.
Jimmy looks over newspaper at Rosie and letter.

JIMMY: You read it to me if you must.

Retreats behind paper.

ROSIE: Oh, there's no must about it. If you're not interested in a letter from your own son, then so be it, Jimmy. So be it!

Rosie puts envelope back in apron pocket.
Pause.

JIMMY: I'm listening.

ROSIE: What's that, Jimmy?

Jimmy sets aside newspaper.

JIMMY: I said I'm listening.

ROSIE: What to, Jimmy? Is there somebody at the door? You go. I'd be afeared to answer it at this time of night.

JIMMY: The letter, Rosie. The letter from Billy. Read the damned thing will ye and get it over with.

ROSIE: Are you sure you wanna hear it, Jimmy? Are you really sure?

JIMMY: Yes. Rosie. I'm sure. Now read it to me, please.

ROSIE: But, Jimmy, are you. . .

JIMMY: Rosie!

Rosie smiling triumphantly, takes out envelope.

ROSIE: For if you don't want to hear it, you don't have to listen. Nobody'll force you. You're free to do what you like in this house, you know that, Jimmy.

JIMMY: That'll be the day.

ROSIE: What was that, Jimmy? Did you hear something strange there?

JIMMY: Not a thing, Rosie. And I'm all ears. Billy's letter. I'm listening.

Rosie removes paper from envelope. Gazes at it without speaking. Dabs her eyes with hankie.

JIMMY: Well, if you're to go on like that woman . . . Rosie. . .

ROSIE: (*Begins reading letter*)
'Dear Ma and Da, just a note to say I arrived in Spain alright. Haven't seen any action yet but expect to very soon. Things are bad for the republic and getting worse, we hear. The Fascists are making quare headway and Christ do they have some hardware. We've heard it! Tell Da, if he'd had half the stuff they have, he'd still be holding the Post Office in Dublin. I'm with a great bunch of people. The first comrade I was introduced to when I got to London was a fellow by the name of Tommy Reid, a sweeney todd from the Shankill, his Da's an out and out Orangeman, would you believe it? But Tommy's the heart of corn and a great man for the cause here in Spain and at home.' (*Rosie stops reading letter*) I wonder is he anything to the Reids your father knew, Jimmy? Remember? What was the name of the wee street they used to live in?

JIMMY: The letter, Rosie. I'm still listening.

ROSIE: God, I can't remember the name of it for the life of me. But it'll come to me before the night's out I'm sure. (*She returns to letter*) '. . . a great man for the cause here in Spain and at home. Tommy and I have kinda teamed up.

Also, in our group is a painter, a woman from London, very posh — I think Big Tommy has taken a shine to her — you should see the way he smiles at her, Ma. Of course he gets a quare sleggin' from me. But posh or not, she's a comrade.'

JIMMY: Women fighting? Making eyes, huh!

ROSIE: Did you say something there, Jimmy?

JIMMY: No. No. Rosie. Go on. Go on.

ROSIE: Must've been the wind again. (*Reading*) 'Another comrade is a poet. A strange quiet big fellow, not long out of Cambridge University.'

JIMMY: Poets and artists! Some war!

ROSIE: What are you slabberin' about, Jimmy? Sure weren't youse tripping over them in 1916 in the Post Office. What about old squint-eyed Padraic, wasn't it a poet? (*Reads letter*) 'He's a member of the Communist Party in England.'

Jimmy nearly chokes.

JIMMY: What dida tell you, Rosie? Reds! Bloody Reds!

ROSIE: (*Reads letter*) 'But tell my Da, he's alright. He has an uncle a bishop. A Protestant bishop. If my Da reads this, Ma, he'll choke on that aul' pipe of his.'

Jimmy is coughing and spluttering.

ROSIE: Are you alright, Jimmy? I thought you were taking a turn there. Your face went that *red*! (*Reads letter*) 'Our other comrade is a great wag altogether. Sammy Cohen. A Jew from within the sound of Bow Bells. A happy-go-lucky sort of fella. Keeps us entertained no end with his banter. He's like somebody from home the way he's always getting the last word in and joking and geaging. Anyway, Ma, I hope this finds you and my Da well. I think of you both from time to time and picture you in the house at home. Don't be worrying. But sure, I know you will even though you'll not let on in front of my Da. I'll write again soon, though it might be a bit difficult if the rumours are right about where we're going in the next few days. Take care and as they say here — SALUD! Love Billy.'

Rosie folds letter and replaces it in envelope.
Silence.
Jimmy has retreated back behind newspaper.

ROSIE: Well, Jimmy? Have you nothing to say?

Pause.

ROSIE: Jimmy!

JIMMY: Painters. Poets. Communists. Jews. Oh, I told him alright. I told him.

Rosie laughs loudly.
Crossfade into two priests.

FATHER O'NEILL: The Republican Government of Spain was elected by the people of Spain. The rebels. The Fascists are of the same kind as our own General Goughs and Carsons. Those today in Ireland who call the rebels in Spain patriots and Christians have proved to be bad judges of patriots and Christians in Ireland. We have had the experience here in Ireland, my dear people, of men being refused the rites of their Church, men who were real patriots — Republicans, my dear people, real Republicans and true patriots like those today fighting against the false patriots, the false Christians — the rebel Fascists in Spain. I hope the Irish people will see through the hypocrisy and sham of these false Christians and rally to the cause of justice in Spain.

Cut to Father Cunningham.

FATHER CUNNINGHAM: And so, my dear people, I urge you to join in a Crusade of prayer, say the family rosary, hear Mass, receive Holy Communion and give generous donations to such organizations as the Christian Front, that the scourge of Communism and Anarchism may be erased forever from the land of Spain and all lands, so that our Christianity will be victorious!

Blackout.

6 SCENE

The Wood of Death. Sound of gun-fire, explosions, aircraft, machine-gun fire, rifle fire. Lighting effects: spot roving. Figures running to and fro, spot picking up figures crawling along on stomachs, comrades at machine-gun positions, general impression of mayhem on battlefront.
Cut.
Silence.
Darkness.

TOMMY: Anybody there?

> *Pause.*

TOMMY: Hello?

BILLY: Tommy?

TOMMY: Who's that?

BILLY: William of Orange. Who'd you think it was, you Protestant eejit? The Pope?

> *Light slowly up, growing in strength*

TOMMY: Are you alright, Billy? Are you in one piece?

BILLY: As much as I ever was. Jesus, that was some attack. . .

FELICITY/VOICE: Tommy? Billy?

TOMMY: Felicity? Where are you?

FELICITY: Over here. . .

TOMMY: Are you alright?

FELICITY: Yes. Yes. I'm alright.

BILLY: Where's Sammy?

Pause.

SAMMY: I'm not here anymore. This ain't a fair fight. Them bleedin' Fascists got all the big guns. It ain't fair. You think things were bad with the Cossacks, mama — well, I got news for you.

BILLY: (*Trips*) Jesus Christ! What was that?

TOMMY: What's the problem, Fenian features?

BILLY: I tripped on something.

TOMMY: Been on the Spanish wine again, eh?

Billy is bending over a body. John's body.

BILLY: Fuck! Sammy, give me a hand here, will you? Bring a sheet or a cloth or something. Tommy, look after Felicity.

SAMMY: (*With sheet*) What is it, Billy? (*Sees John's body*) Oh my God! (*Sammy turns away*)

Felicity approaches.
Tommy tries to restrain her.

FELCITY: If I can fight in a war, I can bear to look at its results, Comrade. Is it John?

Billy and Sammy hesitate.
Felicity steps forward to look at body. As does Tommy. Billy and Sammy cover body with sheet. Tommy brings on a stretcher. Billy and Sammy lift body of John onto stretcher and exit. Tommy and Felicity look after them. Pause.

TOMMY: I'm sorry, Felicity. I didn't mean. . .

FELICITY: It's alright, Tommy. It's just sometimes I get a bit touchy when people try to — protect — me. Never mind, that's me.

TOMMY: Poor John.

FELICITY: Yes. The first of us. I wonder how many more of us will die?

TOMMY: Felicity. . .

FELICITY: You're about to protect me again, Tommy. Women are not as frightened of death and suffering as men seem to think. We know it perhaps better than they do. We give life and then see it taken away. Death is not an abstract for us, Tommy. It is the other side of what makes us women.

Pause.

What are you thinking?

Small pause.

TOMMY: About John. I hardly passed two words with the man, yet I've fought with him now in the same battle for two, three weeks. Watched him lying there dead and I didn't know a bloody thing about him really. Didn't have a proper conversation with him once. He seemed an 'odd' bloke. Strange to the likes of me. Had me wondering what the hell he was doing here. Why he had come? A poet. . .

FELICITY: For the same reason as you have, Tommy.

TOMMY: Aye. I know that, Felicity. But there's still something strange and odd about it.

FELICITY: You mean because he was English and of a certain class and a poet, you find it hard to believe he could have the same ideals and hopes as you.

TOMMY: He was a good comrade. A bloody good comrade. And a brave fighter. I'm not saying anything against him. But yes, I suppose in all honesty, that is what I find odd — he was not of the people-of-no-property, so why should he 'fight' for them?

FELICITY: Doesn't that make it all the more commendable? A privileged background like John's, but willing to fight for the people-of-no-property. Isn't his a greater sacrifice?

TOMMY: Sacrifice is sacrifice, Felicity. But yes, I understand what you mean. (*Pause*) You know, Felicity, ever since we came out here to Spain, I've been thinking a lot along those lines — I mean about who is who and why people do certain things — and I'm coming to the conclusion that a lot of the notions that the likes of Billy and I — well, me definitely — had back home, well, what I'm trying to say is that it comes as a great gunk. . .

FELICITY: Gunk?

TOMMY: (*Laughs*) It comes as a great surprise to me that someone like John who we would have thought of as the class enemy . . . he *was* English, upper class, Cambridge

University, all that . . . but all this has nothing to do with that . . . it has but it hasn't. . . I'm talking back to front alright now, aren't I. . .? But what I mean is, it's not about what you were born into . . . nation, class, whatever . . . but what *you are* . . . here, inside. John was a comrade. He was *my* comrade, in a war against evil . . . in a war for freedom . . . freedom, that's what he had in here . . . that's what he died for. You know, Felicity, I think you were right about that other as well — about women and men and war and death — we are the ones more frightened.

Felicity approaches him. Puts her finger to his lips to silence him and then kisses him. Special spot on John. John smiles.

JOHN: *Adelante, compañeros! Adelante!*

Billy, Tommy, Felicity, Sammy turn in formation.

ALL: *Adelante!*

Blackout

SCENE | 7

Sound and music (sacred music, marching feet, cries, screams — mixed). Dummies of bishops, cardinals, priests, nuns, Franco giving Nazi salute pushed on zig-zag fashion, then formed into line downstage. We see Sammy upstage centre. To Sammy's right — Tommy and Felicity. To Sammy's left — Maria and Billy (getting haircut). During scene, shadowy lights on all, specials on those engaged at time.
Pause.

FELICITY: Tell me about Belfast, Tommy.

TOMMY: Not much to tell, Felicity. It's a city like any other. Lots of poor people. A few rich. But it's home.

FELICITY: Have you any brothers or sisters?

TOMMY: No. There's just me. Me and my Ma and Da. I think when they had me, they both took a look at what had arrived, looked at each other and said, 'that does it — we've had enough.'

FELICITY: What does your father do?

TOMMY: My Da? Aul' Ed? He works in the shipyard. Harland and Woolff.

FELICITY: And your mother?

TOMMY: She, God help her, looks after my Da and me, when I'm there. She's a great woman, my Ma.

FELICITY: And what did you do in Belfast, Tommy? Did you have a job?

TOMMY: Off and on. Before I came to Spain, I was working in Mackies. It's an engineering firm — makes. . .

FELICITY: Did you know Billy in Belfast?

TOMMY: Belfast's a small city, but I'd never come across Billy until I met him in London before we set sail for Paris.

FELICITY: That's funny. I thought you both knew each other — that you had come together from Belfast.

TOMMY: What made you think that, Felicity?

FELICITY: The way you get on together. It's like you're old friends. You're very alike. So alike, you could be brothers.

TOMMY: Well, we are in a manner of speaking — we're comrades.

FELICITY: Yes, I know. But I meant more than that. You do both seem to be from the same family.

TOMMY: The family of workers. The family of Belfast. I *know* what you thought. Belfast people *do* have a strange likeness, even if they're like Billy and me — from opposite sides of the fence.

FELICITY: What fence?

TOMMY: (*Laughs*) I meant being from different religious

backgrounds, Protestant and Catholic.

FELICITY: You're a Protestant, and Billy's a Catholic?

TOMMY: Oh aye, Billy's a pape alright even if he is named after William of Orange! (*Shouts over to Billy*) Aren't you, Billy?

BILLY: What's that, Tommy?

TOMMY: Felicity wants to know whether you're a bloody old Fenian.

BILLY: (*Shouts back*) A Holy Roman, that's me, Comrade. And he's a bigoted aul' orange halion, Felicity!

Felicity smiles somewhat bewildered.
Cut to:

MARIA: Comrade Reid is from your home town?

BILLY: He is, Maria. But he kicks with the wrong foot!

MARIA: He kicks with what? I don't understand.

BILLY: Never mind, Maria. It's too complicated to go into. What's important is that, here in Spain, we are both comrades, together.

MARIA: *Si*. Comrades. I understand. *Compañeros*?

BILLY: (*Almost to himself*) *Compañeros*! What a beautiful word that is. *COM-PAN-EROS*. You know, Maria, you'll not understand this either, but there is something bloody ironic about Tommy and I being '*compañeros*'. It's like, to be real comrades, we had to come to Spain. And there's others here like us. Comrades from different parts of Ireland, some Catholics and some Protestants but all of us *compañeros*. Jesus, if only the people back home could see us now together. If only my father could see this. He was a revolutionary, you know, Maria, my Da. A great man with the explosives was my Da. Learnt the trade fighting the British and has used it since working for a quarry owner who swindled him out of his piece of mountain in Belfast. Swindled by one of his own, a Catholic, and yet for some reason he sees Tommy's lot as the enemy. But Christ, it's the same all over, isn't it? It's the same here in Spain. Those who should be your friends are your enemies and your enemies sometimes turn out to be your friends. Why is it, Maria, for Jesus, it's something

I find hard to understand, why is it that the priests and bishops have turned against the Spanish people when the Spanish people for centuries have fought and died for their Catholic faith?

MARIA: (*Spits*) The Church are Fascists. They side with Franco. They hate the people. But we will make them pay. They are friends to the landowners. But we will take the land — our land — the land of the Spanish people — we will take back what is ours, not theirs.

BILLY: Why did I say I couldn't understand it? It's the same in Ireland. The Church is always against the people. The people die for the Church. Then the Church sides with the enemies of the people.

MARIA: (*Spits again*) Death to the Church. Death to the priests and Bishops and Cardinals. Death to all of them. *Salud, revolutione.*

BILLY: Easy there, comrade. That was nearly death to my ear.

They both laugh at Maria's agitation, nearly resulting in Billy's ear being clipped. Billy stands up, looks in mirror at haircut. Poses.

BILLY: What do you think? I look a handsome revolutionary?

MARIA: The most handsome in Spain.

Cut to:
Sammy writing letter.

SAMMY: Dear Miriam, darling, I'm making use of this break in the fighting to write to my *Liebchen*. My company has withdrawn from the front for a few days for a rest but no doubt we'll be back up there in the thick of it very soon. And Miriam, do we need the rest! We lost one from our company in the last attack by Fascists — posh poet fella name of John. It was Billy found him after the firing had stopped. Billy's this Irish geezer from Belfast, of all places. Right 'eejit' as he would say. There's another like him, Tommy, he's from Belfast as well. And Felicity, London lady, painter. But don't be worrying, Tommy got in there first. Besides, you know your Sammy has eyes only for you. I can see your face as I write that — one of those 'pull the other one' looks on it. But I'm serious, love, I *do* love you and miss you like hell. But thinking about you and writing to you helps. It's not the friendliest place in the world, this I can tell you. These Fascists are right nasty bleeders, but I ain't half glad I came. There's a great feeling amongst the comrades and in a way the feeling's best when we're up at the front. Pounding away at the Fascists for all we're worth. All of us. English. Irish. Americans, Hungarians, Spanish, even some Germans. It's like the good guys from all over the world are here and we're having a go at all the baddies in the world. I can't explain it proper, Miriam, but it's like a real sense of freedom and solidarity. Comradeship. It gives you a good feeling — justifies you — makes you feel alive even though you're surrounded by death and destruction. Does that make sense? I don't know if it does. Miriam, love, what I'd give right now for one of your kisses . . . to caress your soft cheek and look into your big brown Yiddisher eyes. That reminds me, there are other Jews here. I'm not alone. Makes a change. And I had a strange feeling just before we came here. When we were gathering in France before crossing the mountain to Spain . . . it made me think of our ancestors. Yeh, our Jewish ancestors, Miriam. Yours and mine. Travelling. Running. Fleeing from persecution. And all this is like I'm doing it for them. I'm fighting for our people. I'm fighting for the Jews and all the people of the world who had to run or were persecuted. I'm fighting for our freedom. I'm fighting the Fascists for us. Pray God, or whoever, Miriam, that we win here in Spain for it doesn't bear thinking about what'll happen to us all if we lose. We mustn't lose. We can't lose. For if we do, it won't just be Spain'll be a graveyard, it'll be all of Europe. Write to me, Miriam, and send me Mazel. I love you. Sammy.

Others have gathered around Sammy.

TOMMY: (*In a Cod Cockney accent*) What this then, mate? Writing love letters, is it?

BILLY: I didn't know you could write, Sammy.

FELICITY: Don't pay any attention to these two 'eejits', Sammy.

SAMMY: Don't you worry, Comrade, I won't. Just like a couple of Paddies to go to war and spend most of their time courting, ain't it?

Billy and Tommy chase after Sammy.

TOMMY: You'll pay for that, Bow Bells!

Felicity and Maria, arms around each other, laugh at shenanigans of men.

MARIA: Men!

FELICITY: Men? *Boys!*

More laughter.
Light change.

8 | SCENE

Sound of drum, steady slow beat, threatening. Cast rearrange dummies of priests, bishops etc. Stage fills up with other dummies thrown on to represent peasants killed by nationalist forces. Some of the 'bodies' have bayonets stuck in them with attached religious pictures denoting composite photograph of Franco and Christ.
An old woman in shawl enters. She searches amongst the 'bodies'. Pause.
Enter Billy, Tommy, Felicity, Sammy and Maria. Old woman on seeing them falls on knees crying and crossing herself, frightened that they are nationalist forces. Maria goes to her and speaks in Spanish, reassures old woman.
Maria and old woman continue in Spanish.

FELICITY: What is she saying?

MARIA: She says the Fascists came and killed everyone in the village.

Maria speaks to old woman in Spanish who answers.

MARIA: She says she ran away and hid in the hills.

Maria and old woman speak Spanish.

MARIA: She has come back now to search for the bodies of her husband and son.

Maria and old woman speak Spanish.

MARIA: She has brought flowers for their graves. She wants to kneel at the gravesides and say prayers for their souls that they may go to heaven.

Old woman speaks Spanish.

MARIA: She says God will punish those who use his name to do such things.

SAMMY: God? God? Fuck God! Fuck him! What am I saying?

TOMMY: Is everyone else in the village dead?

Maria and old woman speak Spanish.

MARIA: Yes. Everyone. Men. Women. And children. The Fascists they take everyone out and shoot them. The children do not know what is happening to them, but they die just the same. Shot dead.

Maria and old woman speak Spanish.

MARIA: She was lucky, she says.

FELICITY: Lucky?

MARIA: She says God was good. He spared her to tell what happened. To tell the truth of it.

Old woman speaks Spanish.

MARIA: She is pleased to see us. She says God has answered her prayers that some one might come to see. So that she could tell her story.

Old woman speaks Spanish.

MARIA: She wants us to kneel with her. To pray.

TOMMY: To pray?

Felicity goes to Tommy.

MARIA: To pray for her dead husband and her dead son. And for all the people of Spain.

Old woman speaks Spanish.
Pause.

FELICITY: What did she say, Maria?

Pause.

MARIA: She says we must pray. She said we must pray even for the *fasciste*.

TOMMY: Never! Never!

SAMMY: OH GOD!

Old woman speaks Spanish.

MARIA: We must pray that God and His Holy Mother will forgive them for their sins.

Old woman kneels and begins praying in Spanish.
Pause.
Felicity kneels, head bowed.
Pause.
Sammy kneels.
Pause.
Felicity looks appealingly at Tommy. Tommy goes down on one knee, grim-faced and angry. Felicity holds out her hand to Tommy who grasps it tightly.
Billy who has been faced upstage turns, tears streaming down his face.
The voice of old woman praying in Spanish grows louder and louder. Slow fade.

9 SCENE

Lights up.
We see an anniversary celebration going on. General atmosphere of gaiety. Flags. 'Starry Plough'. Sammy ladling out wine from huge bin. Spanish music — Catalonian — Maria doing a Catalan dance

directed at Billy who is preoccupied. Others clapping and stomping feet joining in dance. Irish ceili *music — Tommy and Felicity* ceili *swinging. Sammy does mock Russian dance. Billy remains apart. We see Father O'Neill moving amongst revellers, talking and occasionally dancing a few steps. He then meanders towards raised platform. Father O'Neill bangs on side of wine-bin for attention. Music and dancing gradually stop. All look to Father O'Neill. Pause.*

FATHER O'NEILL: Comrades, I won't interrupt the celebrations for too long. I'm not going to give a sermon. (*Laughter*) But I'd just like to say a few words to you, Comrades, having travelled here from Ireland to be with you in solidarity on this Irish anniversary. I know from talking with some of you that other national anniversaries have been marked by the International Brigade. The 4th of July by our American comrades and Dominion Day by our Canadian comrades, but today it's the turn of the Irish. For on this day in Ireland, a small group of comrades are making their way to the little village of Sallins — to Bodenstown churchyard where the remains lie of a great Irishman and Internationalist, the Father of Irish Republicanism, Theobald Wolfe Tone. A man for whom there were no boundaries. Wasn't it he who said that no longer were there to be the divisions of Catholic, Protestant or Dissenter in Ireland but only Irish men and women? Free Irish men and women. Free from oppression. Free from the yoke of a conquering power. And on this day when Irish comrades here in Spain — taking part in one of the greatest struggles for freedom ever launched by humankind — are feeling perhaps a little sad and nostalgic (no doubt aided by the excellent *vino*), and when their memories are of pint glasses of draught stout served in little pubs by the canal, as they envisage their comrades at home marching today to Tone's tomb, let us hope (dare I say, pray,) that those comrades at home in Bodenstown will spare a thought for them and understand why these Irish comrades are not with them in Ireland. But here in Chabola Valley, a few kilometres from the Ebro River beyond which lie the enemies of freedom, the enemies of men like Wolfe Tone, the enemies of the people of Spain — the Fascists, Comrades.

Let us hope that those standing by Tone's grave today realize that the banner of Tone and James Connolly is flying here on Catalonian soil because Spain's fight is Ireland's fight — because it is the fight of all of us who believe in freedom and democracy. Some of our Irish comrades have already washed this Spanish soil with their blood. Some of you may never return to Ireland. But — let me say it now in memory of those who have died and those of you here still fighting — you are fighting for Ireland's freedom, for Ireland's freedom is Spain's freedom and Spain's freedom is the freedom of the world. I pray God, Ireland will remember to be proud of you. *Salud*!

Father O'Neill raises his glass. Everyone raises glasses.

ALL: *Salud*!

Father O'Neill leads singing of 'The Internationale'. Then he descends from platform and approaches Billy. Music and dancing continue quietly.

FATHER O'NEILL: Billy. How are you?

BILLY: Father O'Neill. (*Pause*) That was a fine speech, Father. Pity those in Ireland weren't around to hear it, for here you're preaching to the converted. It's them at home needs teaching, from what I hear.

FATHER O'NEILL: Things are not good at home, Billy, no, but we mustn't despair. The good are always a small band. So what's new, eh? Christ only had twelve apostles.

BILLY: He seems to have a lot more than twelve here, Father, and all of them Fascists. And in Ireland, he has the Blueshirts. I hear the clergy are going round wearing blue sashes and it's not out of veneration to Our Lady but sucking thumbs to the elbows with Gavan O'Duffy that they're at. And our national poet, Mister William Butler Yeats, has written a marching song for them to dance to. How does it go now?

Billy starts reciting song by Yeats, taunting Father O'Neill. Father O'Neill hits Billy across the face.
Pause.

BILLY: Oh, it's a proud day for Ireland alright, Father O'Neill.

FATHER O'NEILL: It *is* a proud day, Billy. I'm proud. I'm proud of those marching in Bodenstown. I'm proud of the comrades here in Spain. I'm proud of you, Billy.

BILLY: Well, I'm not proud of *your* church, Father O'Neill. For it is *yours*. It's not mine. It was. I was born into it. I was reared in it. I even tried to practise what it preached. But no more, Father O'Neill. No more. For I shall never set foot inside a Roman Catholic Church ever again. Never! Never! Not after what I have seen.

Pause.

FATHER O'NEILL: I take it, Billy, you're referring to the massacre of the people in the village. I heard about it. It was terrible. Terrible things happen in a war when evil forces are unleashed.

BILLY: You're telling me, Father. You're bloody telling me. And they're being unleashed by your bloody superiors. By Bishops and Cardinals. By the bloody Holy Roman Catholic and Apostolic Church! You heard about it? Do you want to know what we saw, Minister of Rome?

FATHER O'NEILL: I can imagine, Billy.

BILLY: Can you? Imagine? Well, I saw it, Father O'Neill. I saw it in front of my own eyes. Bodies! The dead bodies of men, women and children — peasants, Father, poor peasants — butchered, hacked down. All of them, the whole village of them. And you wanna know, Father, what the forces of Christianity did then? Not satisfied simply with killing all and everyone, they stuck little pictures, little 'holy' pictures in the dead bodies. 'Holy' pictures that showed a bleeding Sacred Heart and General Franco hand in bloody hand. That's what I saw, Father O'Neill. Your Church, is — sick. Sick. Sick. . .

Silence.

FATHER O'NEILL: Billy?

BILLY: How can you, Father? How can you bear to wear that collar? For they have spat on it. Made a mockery of it. If you're a comrade, Father O'Neill, take it off. Rip it off and stamp on it. It has no meaning anymore. None! None!

Billy goes for Father O'Neill's collar.

But Father O'Neill ably defends himself and casts Billy aside. Billy is lying on the ground.
Pause.

FATHER O'NEILL: It may be hard to understand, Billy. But it is for the very reasons you give that I must continue to wear it. Because some have brought this collar into disrepute — disgraced it, spat on it, made a mockery of it — does not mean that what it stands for is disgraced. But only those who have worn it. You cannot blame the collar for the action of men.

Billy gets up and approaches Father O'Neill.

BILLY: Well, you listen to this, Father. I can. I can blame it and them. And you can tell that to my Da at home when you see him. Irish patriots of 1916. . .

Billy spits on the ground. He goes off, leaving Father O'Neill standing.
Maria sees Billy go off and follows.
Tommy approaches Father O'Neill. Tommy is slightly drunk.

TOMMY: What's up with Billy, Father? It is 'Father' I address you as, isn't it? You see, I'm not a Taig. Sweeney Todd from the Shankill, me. (*Tommy starts playfully singing 'The Sash my Father wore'. Dancing*)

Felicity joins Tommy and Father O'Neill.

FELICITY: Tommy, what do you think you are doing? Father, forgive him.

FATHER O'NEILL: It's alright, Comrade. I've heard and sung the Sash manys a time myself.

TOMMY: She doesn't know it was the Sash I was singing, Father. She's English and sure what do they know about. . .

FELICITY: Tommy?

TOMMY: How's things at home, Father? What's the news? Isn't it a quare geag the likes of me and Billy being here in Spain? Are you having a drink, Father? This wine's that good it'll be hard to go back to bottles and half'uns.

Cross-fade to upper level.
Billy and Maria.

MARIA: Billy? Comrade?

BILLY: Maria.

MARIA: Are you alright, Comrade?

BILLY: Yes. Yes. Just had a few words with Father O'Neill. That's all.

MARIA: Angry words?

BILLY: Yes. Angry words.

MARIA: I thought so. You disappeared.

       Pause.

MARIA: Can I ask what the angry words were? You know him from *Irlandes*?

BILLY: Yes. It was about home. Ireland. Spain. The Catholic Church. I had a right go at him, the poor bastard. Said he should rip off his collar — denounce it — because of what the Church was doing here.

MARIA: I don't know this Irish priest, your Father O'Neill. But I don't like priests — any of them. None of them are to be trusted. Is he any different?

BILLY: I don't know, Maria. I don't know. He *has* done good work in Ireland. Trying to get us support but. . .

MARIA: A priest is a priest. Even the good ones turn against us, eventually. A priest is a figure of authority and authority crushes our people so we must. . . Authority is not our friend. Authority is our enemy. Any authority.

BILLY: Were you brought up a Catholic, Maria?

MARIA: Of course. This is Spain. My mother still keeps my picture. Me, making my First Holy Communion. It is in her bedroom even though it is a long, long time since I took Communion. (*She laughs*) My mother still hopes. But she will be hoping a long time. I am against religion. Religion is against the people. It is not Communion the people want, but land to grow their own food. Let the priests give Communion to the landowners and let us take the land of the landowners. Today the landowners take both.

BILLY: What made you turn against religion, Maria? Against the Church?

MARIA: Because they are friends with the landowners. The landowners are our enemies. Therefore the priests become our enemies too. They drink together. Get fat together while our people starve. Have you ever seen a hungry priest?

BILLY: No. I haven't. (*Pause*) We have a saying at home in Ireland about priests always looking like they've been well fed and well watered and still they ask the people for money.

MARIA: For God? But what use has God for money? Even if he existed what would he do with it? Buy land?

BILLY: You don't believe in God, Maria? You're an atheist?

MARIA: Aren't you, Comrade?

BILLY: I don't know what I am on that score. I always followed Connolly. . .

MARIA: James Connolly, the socialist revolutionary. He bring freedom to *Irlandés*?

BILLY: Did he? (*Pause*) Connolly said that religion was nothing to do with socialism. Got nothing to do with what a man does on Sunday or where he goes to, if anywhere. He was referring to Catholics and Protestants in Ireland — but all are workers, he said. All are men of labour.

MARIA: The men and women of no property, they are my religion. The revolution!

Pause.

BILLY: Do you think we'll win, Maria? The fascists are strong and many.

MARIA: We must win. We must. The Fascists are strong because our allies are traitors. Traitors to the cause of freedom. But we will defeat them. We have to. If not, it will be better to be dead than live under them.

BILLY: Are you frightened of dying, Maria?

MARIA: Are you, Comrade?

BILLY: Bloody terrified.

MARIA: So am I.

BILLY: We'll have to help each other overcome our fear, Comrade.

Silence.

MARIA: You are very beautiful, *Irlandés.*

BILLY: You are the beautiful one — *Española.*

Maria laughs.

BILLY: What are you smiling at?

Maria continues to laugh.

BILLY: Maria?

MARIA: I'm smiling because we are so. . . so ridiculous. Life is ridiculous. Absurd.

BILLY: It is?

MARIA: Yes. Yes. And us especially.

BILLY: Why so?

MARIA: Because here we are in the middle of a war and yet we still find time to say the most ridiculous things to one another.

BILLY: It's ridiculous . . . to love?

MARIA: I think we should go now to the *ceili.* You haven't danced with me yet.

BILLY: *La Española* gives the orders.

Maria steps towards Billy. She kisses him passionately.

MARIA: I love you, *Irlandés.* Come, we must dance to the revolution!

BILLY: *y L'Espagna!*

Billy lets out ceili yell.
Full lights up on others dancing.
Billy and Maria dance a Catalonian dance.
Slow fade.

10 SCENE

*Sound and lighting effects to create impression of another battle,
e.g. roving spot picking out figures darting about etc.
Cut.
Lights up.
We see Tommy and Felicity. Tommy has arm in sling, obviously
wounded. He is being sent home. Tommy and Felicity locked in an
embrace. They break.*

TOMMY: I'll be back, Comrade.

Felicity nods.

TOMMY: I will. I don't understand why they're sending me home
at all.

FELICITY: You need rest, Tommy. You need looking after. The
wound needs time to heal.

TOMMY: I know who I'd like to change the dressings for me.

They kiss.

TOMMY: You'll look after yourself, Felicity, won't you? I love
you. (*He smiles*) I've never said that to anyone before. My
Ma, yes, but never a *woman*, if you know what I mean.

FELICITY: I love you, Tommy Reid. I *love* you.

They embrace again.

FELICITY: Now, you must be off. Don't let's prolong the agony.

Tommy picks up knapsack.

TOMMY: Write to me, beautiful.

Felicity nods.

TOMMY: I'll be thinking about you — always.

> *Final embrace.*
> *Tommy moves off.*

TOMMY: I'll be back. . .

> *He blows Felicity a kiss and exits.*
> *Hold on Felicity looking straight out. Fade.*

SCENE | 11

Ireland. Sacred music.
Sitting on raised platform at outdoor meeting are General Gavan
O'Duffy, a Lord Mayor and a Monsignor, the latter two wearing
blue sashes. Banner across and hanging from platform reads:
Catholic Young Man's Society. Crowd facing platform hold
placards which read: Christian Front. All are singing 'Faith of our
Fathers' and giving Nazi salute. Tommy is standing a little way off
from crowd downstage close to audience. Platform members sit
after rendition of 'Faith of our Fathers'

VOICE FROM CROWD: Three cheers for the Blueshirts and
General O'Duffy. Hip! Hip!
Hurrah!
Hip! Hip!
Hurrah!
Hip! Hip!
Hurrah!

> *Loud applause and cheering.*
> *Mayor rises to calm crowd. He smiles at O'Duffy who*
> *stands to acknowledge crowd's acclaim.*
> *Silence.*

MAYOR: People of Ireland, we, of the Christian Front in Ireland, are gathered here today to welcome back General O'Duffy and his brave men who have just returned from Spain where they have been fighting the most evil forces ever to threaten the Christian World. The so-called Republican forces who claim that they are fighting for freedom and democracy in Spain when we know that what those same Republican forces are fighting for is the Russian-led Communist take-over of the world. We know, my people, that they are Communists, Reds, Anti-Christs, who butcher and murder and rape nuns, priests and children. They are the red scum who sack churches, defile sacred statues and monuments, who attack and destroy everything that is Catholic, everything that is Christian. But, people of Ireland, rest assured, these evil monsters will not win against the Nationalist forces of God and Our Holy Saviour, Jesus Christ. For we will rout them out and destroy them forever more. We will not submit to the red menace that stalks the countryside of Spain like a club-footed, thong-tailed Satan — for we will crush the serpent under foot until the last drop of venom drips from its fanged, foul mouth. Which is why, people of Ireland, we should be proud today, proud of our part in that fight to crush the Reds, to destroy the beast of Atheism and Communism, proud of men like General Gavan O'Duffy and his brave soldiers in Christ, who return to us today having fought gallantly in that crusade. For that's what it is, people of Ireland; a crusade, a Holy Blessed Christian Crusade like the Crusades of old when the infidel and the Jew were crushed and dispersed to roam the world like the evil beggars they are, we have been represented in that Crusade, we, *Ireland*, have been a participant in that crusade in the person of the General and his men. And I know, people of Ireland, you were there with them, spiritually if not physically. May God Bless the Blueshirts, in the Name of Christ, the King. Thank you. I call upon Monsignor MacNamara to say a few words to you.

Monsignor rises.

MONSIGNOR: In the Name of the Father and of the Son and of the

Holy Ghost Amen. My dear brothers and sisters in Our Lord Jesus Christ, you cannot be a Catholic and a Communist. One stands for Christ and the other for Anti-Christ. Neither can you be an auxiliary of Communism. If you are a Catholic, if you are a Christian, you are on the side of those who are the enemies of Communism. You are on the side of General Gavan O'Duffy and the Blueshirts. You are on the side of General Franco and his forces in Spain. You are on the side of those others in Europe who fight Communism. Italy and Germany would be Communist today but for Mussolini and Hitler. Yes, Hitler persecuted the Church but only to a certain extent, and that was no reason for running him down faced with the great evil that confronts us today. After the General has addressed you, we will offer up to Our Lady, the Mother of God, one decade of the most Holy Rosary, that she may intercede for us to her Most Blessed Son Our Holy Redeemer, Jesus Christ, that he will give succour to us in our desperate hour of peril. In the Name of the Father. . .etc.

ALL: . . . and of the Son and of the Holy Ghost. Amen.

Cheering and shouting as General O'Duffy rises to speak. Silence.

O'DUFFY: A *cairde*. . .

O'Duffy continues speech silently, miming and gesticulating, special light on Tommy who turns to audience.

TOMMY: The truth is, the General and his St Marys Anti-Communist Pipe Band in swirling kilts and flying ribbons were back in Ireland less than six months after it set out on its crusade. It had only taken part in one action . . . when they clashed with a Moorish Unit of Franco's army. The Moors killed four of them. Three others died during a later short period of trench duty. On the one occasion when they were ordered to attack, General Gavan O'Duffy refused because of the imminent risk 'of a huge loss of life'! The Christian Front then demanded to be sent home after they had mutinied against General Gavan O'Duffy himself.

Tommy turns back to face platform.

O'Duffy is still 'speaking' and gesticulating, Hitler-like.
Slow fade.

12 | SCENE

Sound/music — 'The Internationale'. Very loud. This is played
throughout the execution scene during which the 'dummies' of
priests, bishops and nuns are lined up for execution and rape.
Sound of firing squad. 'Dummies' fall dead. Cut music and sound.
Cross-fade to Billy, Maria and Sammy who it is obvious have
witnessed the execution scene. Sammy is traumatized. He prays in
Hebrew interspersed with mutterings of the Kaddish. The delivery
of his Hebrew prayers speeds up until at the end of scene it is
frenetic. Felicity enters during course of scene.
Pause.

MARIA: You're a sentimentalist, Comrade Billy. A religious sentimentalist.

BILLY: Is that what I am *Comrade*? And what are you? What are you, *Comrade*?

MARIA: A revolutionary!

BILLY: Is that so? Is that what you are? And tell me, Comrade, is it a revolutionary act to execute priests and rape nuns? Is that what all this is about? Is *that* we have just witnessed, revolution? That was a nun for Christ's sake! A nun! I don't remember James Connolly saying anything about the path to socialism being strewn with violated nuns. *That*, comrade was nothing but an act of barbarity!

MARIA: You are being hysterical, Comrade.

BILLY: Am I? Well, maybe we need a bit more hysteria around

here if that's the case. Maybe we need a few more Sammys around here. Look at the state of him. Look at Sammy, Comrade. Now go on, tell me, is that the face of victorious revolution? Is that the look of a proud revolutionary?

MARIA: He is a little shocked. He will recover in time.

BILLY: *A little shocked?* I like your language, Comrade. Recover in time? Look at him for Christ's sake. He is completely and utterly fucked. Sammy Cohen will never be the same again. Sammy Cohen has been driven *mad* by your revolution. By your condoning and excusing this butchery.

MARIA: I repeat, Comrade, you are being hysterical. Worse, you are being hypocritical. This is a war, Comrade. You have not forgotten that. It is not an Irish fist fight.

Exchange of looks.

MARIA: There are no buts in war. No second thoughts. If we had had second thoughts yesterday with those Falangists, we'd be dead today. And the revolution would be dead.

BILLY: It *is* dead, Comrade. It died with that nun.

MARIA: That nun, Comrade, that holy Catholic nun was a Fascist! She was the same Fascist nun we also saw yesterday drilling Spanish children in the Nazi salute. Real Catholic nuns are not Fascists. They do not spread the word of Jesus Christ by indoctrinating children to give the Falange salute. She was a Fascist. She deserved to die.

BILLY: And I suppose she deserved the bloody violation before her execution as well. What heading of the revolutionary handbook does *rape* come under? (*Pause*) *Well?*

Pause.

MARIA: Such excesses sometimes. . .

BILLY: *Excesses?* 'Can't be helped', is that what you were going to say, Comrade? Yes. It was — 'unfortunate'. A little 'over-reaction' maybe. A little too much revolutionary zeal and fervour, perhaps. . .

MARIA: Billy?

BILLY: Oh no, Comrade. Oh, no. Don't you try to soft soap me with your 'Billys'. But you listen to me, Comrade. I meant

what I said. *The revolution is dead*. It's certainly *dead* for
Comrade Billy Robinson. *Dead. Dead. Dead.*

Enter Felicity.

FELICITY: Billy? Maria? What's going on here? What's wrong
with Sammy? Why's he. . .

BILLY: *La Española* will explain it all to you, Felicity. *La
Española* has all the answers!

*Felicity looks inquiringly at Maria who keeps her eyes
steadily on Billy.*

MARIA: And *Irlandés* is still in the grip of his Mother Church!

Billy and Maria stare at each other.
Felicity looks from one to the other.
Sammy's praying reaches its climax.
Slow fade on others. Hold on Sammy. Blackout.

13 SCENE

*Sound and lighting effects . . . another battle. Felicity is behind a
large machine-gun frantically firing. Impression is of a furious
battle.*
Cut sound.
*Special light on Felicity. She has been shot: face mask-like, mouth
open, eyes wide and staring.*
Cross-fade to Tommy. Sound: slow drum beat.

TOMMY: I came back, Felicity. I said I would.

Special light on Felicity's ghost.

FELICITY: I knew you would, Tommy. I knew you would come
back to me.

TOMMY: I had to. Things are bad at home. Very bad. Ireland has disgraced herself, Felicity. This is where I have to be. 'I' have to be. But I came back also for you — for you, Felicity.

FELICITY: I know, Tommy. I'm sorry I'm not here to greet you. I *was* waiting for your return.

TOMMY: I love you, Felicity.

FELICITY: I love you, Tommy.

TOMMY: I've loved you since — since that night we talked in that barn at the foot of the Pyrenees before. . .

FELICITY: Before we arrived in the future. But there is to be no future for me, Tommy. It saddens me to say, I don't think there is to be a future in Spain. We are losing, Tommy. We have lost. The revolution has been defeated. But even in defeat, Tommy, even in death, I am a little happy. I was here. I fought. I loved. *I was here.* Tell them I was here, Tommy. Go back and tell them.

TOMMY: I will remember you always, Felicity. Always. It is cruel that I should return, now to be sent home. They are sending all the Comrades of the International Brigade back home. I wanted you to come home with me, Felicity.

   Pause.

FELICITY: I am home, Tommy. The Olive Groves are where I shall live always. There are many of us here. I shall not be lonely. You must not be lonely, Tommy. Remember us. Remember we shall always be with you. I will be with you, always. *Salud compañero. Salud!*

   Light out on Felicity.

TOMMY: My love.

   Music: Spanish love song.
   Slow fade.

14 SCENE

Billy and Sammy by the roadside. By their appearance we can tell they have been travelling and sleeping rough. Billy is hungrily eating oranges. Sammy sits rocking himself to and fro.

BILLY: Eat, Sammy. You must eat. We won't make it, Sammy, if you're weak.

Sammy, oblivious, rocks to and fro and chants Hebrew prayer.

BILLY: Eat, Sammy. Please. We'll be home soon. Away from here. Away from Spain. We'll be out of hell soon, Sammy. Home, Sammy. You'll be home in London. In Cockneyland, Sammy. Soon. Soon.

Sammy increases pace of rocking and volume of praying.

BILLY: Will you for fuck's sake, eat, Sammy? And stop making that bloody noise.

Sammy's praying gets louder and louder.

BILLY: Stop it, Sammy. Stop it.

Billy tries to prevent Sammy chanting but to no avail.

BILLY: Shut up, Sammy. Shut up. You'll have the Fascists on top of us if you don't give over that ranting. If not the Fascists then the 'revolutionaries'. Either way, we'll be goners, Sammy. Please! Please!

Sammy's chanting becomes quieter. Then he suddenly stops.

SAMMY: They're here.

Sammy jumps up rigid as Fascist forces enter to surround him and Billy, guns trained upon them both.

SAMMY: They're here.

Sammy breaks through the Fascists to run away. A Fascist officer turns and shoots Sammy in the back as he runs. Sammy falls. The officer goes to Sammy's body. He fires three more times into Sammy's body.

GESTAPO OFFICER: Dirty Jew! (*He spits*)

And with his foot rolls Sammy's body over.
Officer turns to Billy.

OFFICER: Are you, too, a dirty Jew?

Billy does not answer. He stares at the body of Sammy.

OFFICER: Answer me. Are you a Jew-boy, 'Comrade'?

Billy still stares at Sammy's body.
Officer hits Billy across face with butt of revolver.
Officer gives Nazi salute.
Billy stares at Gestapo officer.
Officer aims revolver at Billy's head.
A second officer intervenes.

SECOND OFFICER: No! Our orders are to capture alive for the purpose of exchange.

Officers exchange looks.
First officer lowers revolver and replaces in holster. Then approaches close to Billy's face and spits at him and knees him in groin.
Billy is then dragged ritualistically around stage.
Light change.
Billy is dumped in cell.
Exit officers.
Sound/cell door banging.
Light change.
Billy lying in cell.
Pause.
Sound of feet on stone floor.
Cell door opening, then sound of feet.
Silence.
Sound of firing squad.
Pause.

Sound of feet on stone floor.
Cell door opening.
Sound of feet.
Silence.
Sound of firing squad.
Pause.
Sound of feet on stone floor.
Sound of door opening.
Enter officers.
Lighting effect: shadows enlarged (film noir).
We see figures beating Billy with sticks.
They stop, officers leave.
Sound of door banging, sound of feet, silence.
Billy crawls towards journal, picks it up, sees Redemption, utters a mixture of hysterical laughter and tears, rolls over and remains frozen still.
Silence.
Sound of feet on stone floor.
Sound of door opening.
Enter Father Gambara, a Jesuit.
Sound of door closing.
Pause.
Father Gambara stands over Billy.
Eventually Billy looks up at him.

FATHER GAMBARA: Are you ready to confess, my son?

Billy rolls over uttering a weird laugh.
Blackout. Simultaneous echoes of the weird laugh. Cut.

Farewell to the International Brigade. Sad music. Farewell banners, flowers, bouquets, cheering and songs.
Maria is on upper level. As she begins to speak, Tommy turns to face audience so that Maria and he are in a direct line.

MARIA: Comrades, it is a hard task, one of the hardest, to say, in a few words — farewell. Farewell to the heroes of the International Brigades.

TOMMY: Some heroes. . .

MARIA: A feeling of sorrow and sadness grips our throats. Sorrow for those leaving. Sorrow for those soldiers of idealism.

TOMMY: Tired soldiers. Disenchanted soldiers. Disillusioned soldiers. Dead soldiers.

MARIA: Sorrow for those exiles from their countries who out of love came to fight for *L'España*.

TOMMY: Returning to their countries to be 'exiles' there.

MARIA: Sorrow for those who will stay here forever beneath Spanish soil.

TOMMY: John Cornwall. Felicity Smythe. And those whose whereabouts are not known. Sammy Cohen. Billy Robinson.

MARIA: We grieve in our hearts for all. You came to us from all peoples, all races. You came to Spain. You fought with heroism and a spirit of sacrifice.

TOMMY: And with fear.

MARIA: In Jarama.

TOMMY: Guadalajara.

MARIA: Bunete.

TOMMY: Belchite.

MARIA: Levante.

TOMMY: And on the River Ebro.

MARIA: Comrades, for the first time in the history of the people's struggles. . .

TOMMY: Poor people. Lost struggle.

MARIA: There has been the grand spectacle of the International Brigade helping to save democracy and freedom in our land of Spain.

TOMMY: A grand 'tragedy'.

MARIA: Communists. Socialists. Anarchists. Republicans. People of many and different and no religions.

TOMMY: Taigs and Prods.

MARIA: Inspired by a love of liberty they came and offered themselves to us. Banners of Spain, salute these heroes.

TOMMY: I am not a hero.

MARIA: Lower Spain's banners in honour of their martyrs. Our martyrs.

TOMMY: Felicity did not want to be a martyr.

MARIA: People of Spain. Remember them. Speak to your sons and daughters. Speak to the future of the International Brigades.

TOMMY: We thought we had arrived in the future.

MARIA: Comrades of the International Brigades, today, for political reasons, reasons of State, you are being sent back home.

TOMMY: A part of us can never leave.

MARIA: Go proudly. You are history. You are legend.

TOMMY: We are lonely.

MARIA: We shall not forget you.

TOMMY: Our memories are here.

MARIA: And when the Olive Tree puts forth its leaves of peace again. . .

TOMMY: We can have no peace ever again.

MARIA: Come back. Come back to us. For you will find always the love and gratitude of the entire Spanish people awaits you as our Spanish hearts now as one cry out: *Long live the International Brigades!*

TAPE/ALL: *Long live the International Brigades! Long live the International Brigades! Long live the International Brigades!*

Music 'The Internationale'
Maria descends from platform.
Walks up to Tommy.

MARIA: Comrade?

> *Tommy turns to face Maria.*
> *Sad music.*

MARIA: Adios, Comrade.

> *Maria offers her hand, Tommy holds it.*
> *Pause.*

MARIA: If you ever see Billy . . . tell him . . . tell him. . .

> *Maria kisses Tommy on both cheeks, then exits hurriedly.*
> *Tommy turns back to face audience.*

TOMMY: Adios . . . *l'Espagna.*

> *Pause. Blackout. Sound of slow drumbeat.*

16 | SCENE

Belfast, Ireland. Home of the Robinson family. We see Rosie and Jimmy, Tommy Reid and Father O'Neill.

JIMMY: He's no bloody son of mine if he ran away. I didn't agree with him going in the first place but if you commit yourself, then that's it. You take what comes. You carry out the job of work you set out on. You don't turn your back on it. You don't become a bloody traitor. You don't turn renegade and desert. You don't turn yellow.

TOMMY: Mr Robinson, I don't think Billy turned yellow. I was there with him — not at the time of the incident — but I fought beside your son. He was a brave man. Courageous. Generous.

JIMMY: So why did he run then, eh? Why did he take himself off?

ROSIE: Jimmy, the fella's just told you what happened. For God's sake, can you not. . .?

JIMMY: Can I not what, Rosie? Can I not accept that my own flesh and blood is a coward?

TOMMY: He was not a coward, Mr Robinson. He was an idealist who could not bear to see those ideals 'dirtied', as he saw it.

JIMMY: And what did he expect? A bloody Sunday picnic? Christ, it was a war he was fighting in. A bloody civil war and they're dirty — the dirtiest! I know, son, I've been through one. I fought in a civil war and I'm not proud of some of the things I did in it, but I did them. I had to. That's what being a soldier is all about. Killing! Killing the enemy! And if sometimes it's confusing who the enemy is, you kill first and ask the questions afterwards. Conscience is a luxury of peace-time, no matter what the likes of Father O'Neill here will tell you.

FATHER O'NEILL: Our consciences, Mr Robinson, are not something we can turn off and on like a light switch. They remain burning all the time, even when we 'think' we may have ignored them. You said yourself, there are things *you* did in '22 that you are not particularly proud of. If that's not conscience speaking. . .

Father O'Neill shrugs.
Jimmy looks at Father O'Neill but says nothing.

ROSIE: You haven't been able to find out anything more, Father, about what happened to our Billy?

FATHER O'NEILL: No, Mrs Robinson, I haven't, but I'll keep trying. I don't want to falsely raise your hopes but I believe he was probably picked up by Franco's forces and imprisoned.

ROSIE: You think he's still alive then, Father?

FATHER O'NEILL: I don't know, Mrs Robinson. Nothing can be certain in Spain anymore, but Billy will be of greater use to Franco as a hostage to exchange for Nationalist prisoners than. . . My guess, my hope, is that Billy is now in prison in Burgos.

TOMMY: Do you think they will release him, Father? In exchange I mean.

FATHER O'NEILL: I hope. I pray.

Mrs Robinson takes out rosary beads from apron pocket.

ROSIE: Sometimes, it's very difficult, Father O'Neill, to hope — to pray. For the odds always seem stacked against us. I dunno, but yon fella called evil always seems to win hands down in the battle with good. Even those, like our Billy and Tommy here, who went to Spain to fight on the side of good end up doing. . . You know, Father, I used to think it was simple. Love thy neighbour as thyself, that's what I was taught as a wee child growing up. But how do we do it, Father? How do we love? And does it? Does love always mean sacrifice? Jesus on the Cross. Jimmy's friends in

1916. The people of Spain. Tommy's English girl. Our Billy. Love demanding sacrifice after sacrifice.

FATHER O'NEILL: (*He kneels*) Let us pray, Mrs Robinson, that this be the last sacrifice.

ROSIE: Somehow, Father, I fear it won't be, human beings being as they are.

FATHER O'NEILL: We can only pray, Mrs Robinson.

ROSIE: Sometimes, Father, it feels useless to pray against evil. But I suppose it's all we have in the end. Prayer. We end by whispering prayers in the ears of the dead and hope that those left will do the same for us.

Pause.

FATHER O'NEILL: In the Name of the Father and of the Son and of the Holy Ghost. Amen. Our Father, who art in heaven. . .

ROSIE: Give us this day our daily bread . . . etc.

Jimmy kneels beside Rosie.
Then Tommy kneels. Silently.

FATHER O'NEILL: Hail Mary full of Grace, the Lord is with Thee. . .

ROSIE/JIMMY: Holy Mary Mother of God Pray for us sinners . . . etc.

As Rosie, Jimmy, Father O'Neill and Tommy kneel praying, lights come up on Maria standing on upper level holding Spanish flag.
Special light comes up on Billy in prison cell.
We hear voice of Adolf Hitler at Nuremberg Rally: 'Sieg Heil! Sieg Heil!.' Sound of marching feet etc.
Builds to crescendo drowning out the voices of those gathered in the Robinson home.
Hold image and sound.
Cut. Blackout.

THE GERMAN CONNECTION

A play
in 2 acts

THE GERMAN CONNECTION was first performed in
November 1986 at the Young Vic Theatre, London.

CAST

TOMMY REID/FIRST MAN	Matthew James McAuley
JIMMY ROBINSON	Toby Byrne
ROSIE ROBINSON	Annie Raitt
BILLY ROBINSON	Mike Dowling
MIRIAM JACOBS	Julia Swift
RACHEL JACOBS	Nathalie Harris
SECOND MAN	John Axon

The play was directed by Julia Pascal.

CHARACTERS

TOMMY REID
JIMMY ROBINSON
ROSIE ROBINSON
BILLY ROBINSON
MIRIAM JACOBS
RACHEL JACOBS

TWO MEN

Belfast 1941. Home of the Robinsons, working class Catholics in Belfast. We see Jimmy Robinson, his son Billy and Tommy Reid.

JIMMY: So you're joining up, is that what you're telling me, Tommy Reid? Off to fight in England's war because some upper class English floosie appears to you in a vision. Well, aren't you the right bloody eejit. What's England ever done for the likes of you or your kind?

TOMMY: Felicity was her name, Mister Robinson.

JIMMY: What?

TOMMY: Felicity was the name of the English woman who died fighting in Spain, Mister Robinson.

JIMMY: Aye. Well. I know you were soft on . . . Felicity. . .

TOMMY: I loved her.

JIMMY: Aye. Love? Love? Well, any road it's no reason to go off now and join the British army.

TOMMY: I have other reasons, Mister Robinson. There's a war on against the Fascists . . . the same Fascists Billy and I fought against in Spain.

JIMMY: Is *that* what our Billy was doing in Spain?

Exchange of looks.

TOMMY: *Yes.* It was, Mister Robinson.

JIMMY: Tell me something, Tommy Reid. Why is it always that you Protestants can't wait to run off and fight for England but when it comes to Ireland's troubles youse are nowhere to be found? What sort of a hold does England have on you? . . . that you side with her and not the land that gave you birth . . . the land you live in.

TOMMY: Mister Robinson, there's nobody in this room more Irish than myself. Billy knows, and you should know, I'm against the partition of this country. I'm a socialist by committment, a Protestant by accident of birth. I'm a Republican, Mister Robinson, and so was many an Irish Protestant . . . I don't have to remind you of that surely — Wolfe Tone, Robert Emmett —

JIMMY: But you're still going to fight in England's war. You can't wait to put on the uniform of the Empire. The Empire that has oppressed this country for centuries.

TOMMY: Wolfe Tone wore a French uniform, Mister Robinson. . .

JIMMY: The Empire, Tommy Reid, I fought against so that we might be free . . . you now are going to fight for that Empire.

TOMMY: I'm not joining the British army to fight for any Empire, Mister Robinson. I'm joining because the war in Spain is continuing now all over Europe.

JIMMY: And if England had helped you in your fight in Spain there might not be a war in Europe now. Didn't you and Billy yourselves say that your so-called allies, your democratic friends, sold youse out?

TOMMY: That's as maybe, Mister Robinson. The fact is, that England has now declared war on the Nazis. People and countries always come late in realizing what needs to be done. Besides this isn't England's war . . . this is the war of all of us who are Anti-Fascist.

JIMMY: Well, by Christ, it isn't Ireland's war. We want nothing to do with it. Let England get on with it herself this time. She's declared war. Let her do the fighting.

BILLY: And England's trouble is Ireland's gain . . . like in 1916, Da?

JIMMY: Yes. Yes. Like in 1916. Why not? We'll give England plenty of trouble yet, given half the chance. The enemies of England are the friends of Ireland. Always were.

Always will be.

TOMMY: We keep some strange company in that case, Mister Robinson.

BILLY: Do you count Adolf Hitler as a friend of Ireland then, Da?

JIMMY: If he's an enemy of England. . .

TOMMY: Jesus Christ, do you realize what you're saying?

BILLY: And this from a man who fought with the idealists of 1916, who fought for the freedom of a small nation against the Empire? Do you know what Hitler thinks of small nations, Da? Ask Czechoslovakia!

JIMMY: I know what England thinks of them. Poor little Belgium. We must defend her . . . join the British Army, be a Redmondite volunteer, and then after the war is over, we'll give *you*, little Ireland, your freedom. Like hell, she did! She did everything in her power to crush us . . . unsuccessful at starving us to death seventy years before, she tried to blast us into extinction. And she would have done, if we'd had to rely on the likes of the Tommy Reids of this world . . . for instead of fighting for their own, they were too busy running off to foreign lands to fight for England and look what happened to them. Muddy graves at the Somme that's what happened to them. And the same, m'boy, will happen to you, if you insist on donning the uniform of your country's oppressor. Assuming, that is, you believe Ireland is your country.

Small pause.

BILLY: He wouldn't want it if it's peopled with narrow-minded bigots the likes of you, Da.

JIMMY: Hoho! Would you listen to 'our Billy'. Veteran yellow-belly of the Spanish Civil War. The Republican who ran. The revolutionary socialist with no stomach for the revolution. The soldier who doesn't want to kill. So what would your Orange friend here want? Ireland peopled with . . . cowards the likes of you and traitors like himself? I notice 'our Billy' you're not volunteering yourself to fight Hitler and the Nazis . . . is that for political reasons or are you just shit-scared?

Pause.
Enter Rosie.

ROSIE: Oh, have I got great news. God, you know, I'm that excited I don't know whether I'm coming or going. And it's all thanks to a chance meeting with Father O'Neill. I bumped into him coming out of the chapel. Well, he told me about how they were evacuating some people from England, women and children mostly, and how they were looking for families to take these people in, and he asked me was I interested. Well, sure I leapt at the chance . . . for sure the company would be great for me during the day . . . what with you men out at work all day. And two pairs of hands is better than one, not that I'd want the poor cratur to do much. It was the company and crack that appealed to me and sure I thought wouldn't it be great to have a child about the house again . . . there's nothing like having a youngster around to keep you young and on your toes and God love them, isn't it a great opportunity to perform a Christian act . . . they're having it rough over in England you know, what with the bombings and blackouts and that. Anyway, I told Father O'Neill, yes. He asked shouldn't I check it with you, Jimmy, but I said I'd never in twenty-odd years of married life checked anything with you and I wasn't going to start now. And that besides, although you could be a bit grumpy in your way, you'd be delighted at the thought of being able to help and Father O'Neill said, yes that was true, for there wasn't a better member of Our Lady's Confraternity than Jimmy Robinson. I didn't laugh . . . honestly . . . I didn't, Jimmy.

Rosie looks straight into Jimmy's face, then from Jimmy to Billy and Tommy.
Pause.

ROSIE: She arrives tomorrow.

Hold. Blackout.

Belfast docks.
We see Miriam Jacobs and her daughter Rachel. They anxiously look around, then sit on suitcase to wait. Enter Rosie. Miriam stands up.

MIRIAM; Mrs Robinson?

ROSIE: Yes.

MIRIAM: I'm Miriam Jacobs.

ROSIE: Miriam, love. How are you doing? Pleased to meet you. I'm Rosie — never mind that Missus nonsense. And who's this little beauty?

She lifts child.

What's your name?

RACHEL: Rachel.

ROSIE: Rachel! What a beautiful name. A beautiful name for a beautiful little girl. And what age are you, Rachel?

RACHEL: Seven and a half.

ROSIE: Seven and a half. Very important that half, isn't it, when you're that young. And when will you be eight? When's your birthday?

Rachel looks inquiringly at mother.

MIRIAM: March the first. Tell the lady, Rachel.

Rachel looks shyly at Rosie who hugs her close and kisses her, then sets her down.

ROSIE: Is this all your luggage, Miriam? You've got everything?

MIRIAM: Yes. Just these two.

ROSIE: Right. Give that one to me and we'll be off. Are you going to take my hand, Rachel?

Rachel looks at Mother.

MIRIAM: Take Rosie's hand, Rachel.

ROSIE: That's a girl. And off we go to Rosie's house. Are you tired, Rachel, after your long journey?

Rachel shakes her head.

ROSIE: How was the crossing, Miriam?

MIRIAM: Fine. It was a little rough at one point during the night, but she slept through it, thankfully.

ROSIE: That was good. And you weren't sick or anything yourself?

MIRIAM: No.

ROSIE: Good. Well, that's something. For I hear tell that aul Irish Sea of ours can be right and crotchety when she wants . . . mind you, I wouldn't know for I've never been across her. Did you know that Rachel? Rosie hasn't been on a big boat like you have been. No. The only sailing Rosie's ever done has been across on the ferry from Strangford to Portaferry. You'll have to tell Rosie, Rachel, what it's like on a really big boat and how it is to sail all the way from England to Ireland . . . will you do that? Will you tell Rosie about your adventure?

Rachel nods and smiles at Rosie happily.

ROSIE: It's great to have you, Miriam. You're more than welcome.

Rosie indicates that Miriam should link her arm.

MIRIAM: Thank you Mrs . . . *Rosie.* We're happy to be here!

Exit and blackout.

Kitchen of Robinson home. Rosie is clearing dishes from table into scullery after meal. Enter Miriam.

MIRIAM: Can I help you with those?

ROSIE: You'll do no such thing. I'm just clearing them into the scullery. I'll red them up afterwards. Is the child asleep?

MIRIAM: Yes.

ROSIE: God love her. She must be exhausted. That's a very beautiful child you have there, Miriam. She's a delight.

MIRIAM: She can have her less delightful moments, I assure you.

ROSIE: Can't we all, and without the excuse of being children. Did she get enough to eat do you think?

MIRIAM: Plenty. Yes, thanks.

ROSIE: And yourself? Would you like another drop of tay? Tea?

MIRIAM: No. No, thanks. I'm fine, Rosie. Thank you. Please let me do something. I don't want to. . .

ROSIE: You don't want to do nothing. You must be exhausted yourself. Do you want to go up and have a lie down?

MIRIAM: Later, perhaps. But I'm fine now.

ROSIE: Whatever you wish. Just say the word.

MIRIAM: You're very kind, Rosie. I'm most grateful.

ROSIE: Nonsense. Now, sit down there by the fire and give me a bit of your crack.

MIRIAM: Pardon?

ROSIE: Conversation. A bit of crack we call it. Oh, before long

we'll have you talking as if you were born and reared in
Belfast town.

Miriam laughs. Rosie sits down opposite her.

ROSIE: Now, tell me all about yourself, for I'm busting to hear.
You're not 'ordinary' English, am I right?

MIRIAM: No. I'm Jewish.

ROSIE: I thought so. For when you said your name and then the
child's — Rachel — I thought to myself that doesn't fit
into the normal categories we have here for sorting people
out by their handles. But you'll discover that for yourself
before long as well. Anyway, I thought . . . Jacobs . . .
Miriam Jacobs . . . Rachel Jacobs . . . well it's not
Catholic and it's not Protestant, so it must be Jewish. But
here's me rattling on when it's yourself should be doing
the talking. Go on, tell me about yourself, Miriam.

Miriam smiles, embarrassed.

MIRIAM: I don't know where to begin.

ROSIE: Your parents. Tell me about your parents.

MIRIAM: My parents? Are both dead, Rosie.

ROSIE: I'm sorry. I should've realized. . .

MIRIAM: No. No . . . It's alright, Rosie. I like to talk about them.
Makes them feel . . . close, if you know what I mean.

ROSIE: I can understand that, Miriam. What were their names?

MIRIAM: My mother was Esther. My father Nathan. Jacobs was
their surname too. You see, I didn't have to change my
name when I married.

ROSIE: Lucky you. Mine was Magee. And to this day I resent
being called Robinson — it's so . . . God forgive me but
I'm an awful bigot sometimes . . . you see Jimmy's father
was a Protestant from the Shankill Road . . . that's
another thing you'll learn about before long . . . certain
areas in Belfast are Catholic and others are Protestant.

MIRIAM: Like ghettos.

ROSIE: The very same. Anyway, Jimmy's Da was a Prod but God
love him he turned alright . . . converted . . . to marry
Jimmy's mother, Mary — Mary O'Hanlon. God, Miriam,
hasn't history a funny way of behaving? Jimmy's father

was a Protestant . . . married a Catholic . . . Jimmy was brought up a Catholic . . . fought in 1916, the Easter Rising that is . . . and so the son of a Shankill Road man became a Fenian!

ROSIE: A Fenian?

MIRIAM: Oh, never mind that now, I'll explain it to you later. Go on, *you* were telling me about *your* history. Your mother and father, Esther and. . .

MIRIAM: Nathan. . .

ROSIE: Nathan Jacobs. And where were they from, Miriam? Were they born in England?

MIRIAM: No. They were both from Roumania.

ROSIE: Roumania? That's an awful romantic sounding place to me. Rou-mania!

MIRIAM: My mother and father, I think, were pretty romantic. They were very deeply in love. My mother was quite a beauty. She was blonde with blue eyes . . . not the usual Jewish dark looks . . . but my father was dark. Dark hair. Brown eyes. I take after him as you can see. And I've got his size as well. Not exactly tall. My mother was taller. When I was little I used to think she towered over him. She was only an inch bigger than him but it seemed more to me then. She nearly always wore flat or low-heeled shoes when they went out together. She knew it made my father uncomfortable to be thought of as 'the small man'.

ROSIE: The things we women do to bolster the vanity of our menfolk! But why did they leave Rou-mania, Miriam?

MIRIAM: Pogroms. Persecution. Not of them directly but Jews weren't having a particularly good time, so they decided to leave.

ROSIE: Before it was too late. And they went to England?

MIRIAM: Yes. Manchester.

ROSIE: It doesn't sound as romantic as Rou-mania.

MIRIAM: (*Laughs*) No. It's not. Not that I have ever been to Rou-mania.

ROSIE: And that's where you were born, Manchester?

MIRIAM: Yes. It's ironic, you know, Rosie, but my mother

wanted to go to Germany and not England. Her family had originally been from Germany before going to Roumania, but my father had some family connections in England. In Manchester — they were in textiles — and so that's where they went. My mother hated it. She couldn't speak English very well, you see. She had few friends and she hankered after either returning to Roumania or going to Germany.

ROSIE: Your father, I think, made the right decision. Germany's not a nice place these days, for anyone . . . and certainly not for Jewish people.

MIRIAM: It's strange, you know, but part of me is glad that both my parents died before they could see the rise of the Nazis and what's happening in Germany today. It would certainly have killed my mother . . . broken her heart . . . for though she was born in Roumania, I think she felt very German. She spoke German. (*Smiles*) She looked German. Blonde. Blue eyes. Poor mother . . . it was good she went when she did.

Pause.

ROSIE: When did she die?

MIRIAM: Four years ago. A year after my father. My father died of a heart attack. Business was not good and he had a lot of worry. He wasn't really a businessman — far too casual and generous for the business world. He used to loan huge amounts of money to people knowing he would never see it, or them, again. He loved singing. I think he wanted to be a *chazan*.

ROSIE: A what, Miriam?

MIRIAM: A *chazan*. It's the man who sings in the synagogue. But it's not a job that pays well when you have a wife and family to keep.

ROSIE: And your mother?

MIRIAM: She died of pneumonia. She caught a chill and it developed into pneumonia. She didn't last long. She couldn't understand why it rained so much in Manchester. She used to say that God must be punishing Manchester for something in its past which is why he never let the sun shine upon it. But I think she wanted to die. She missed my father terribly. Life for her was her life with Nathan and, though she had children (I have a brother), children are no substitute for a husband. I remember catching her once, Rosie, standing by the window of the front room gazing out at that Manchester rain which was streaming down the windows . . . tears trickling down her face and she murmuring my father's name . . . Nathan. . . Where are you? Why have you left me?

Miriam begins to sob, Rosie goes to her to comfort.
Silence.
Enter Billy.

BILLY: Oh, you're in, Ma. I thought there was nobody here the house was that quiet. (*Sees Miriam*) I'm sorry. . .

Miriam moves away from Rosie, her back to Billy, she dabs her eyes and tries to appear not embarrassed.

ROSIE: Billy, this is Miriam. Miriam, this is my son, Billy.

BILLY: Hello, Miriam.

Miriam turns. Billy steps forward to shake hands. Miriam hesitates. They shake hands.

MIRIAM: Pleased to meet you, Billy.

Hold look and handshake.
Slow fade.

SCENE   4

Robinson's kitchen.
Miriam with Rachel, drawing a picture.

RACHEL: Mummy, when's daddy coming to live with us in Rosie's house?

Small pause.

MIRIAM: Soon. I hope, darling. Very soon.

Small pause.

RACHEL: Mummy? Why did daddy go away?

MIRIAM: He had to, sweetheart. You see there's a war on, and your daddy. . .

RACHEL: What's a war, mummy?

MIRIAM: A war is. . .

VOICE OF TOMMY: Hello! Anybody home? Missus Robinson?

Enter Tommy.

TOMMY: Oh, I'm sorry. I was looking for Rosie. Or Billy?

MIRIAM: Missus Robinson is out. And Billy's at work. (*Pause*) Would you like to wait?

TOMMY: Thanks. I'm not disturbin' you, am I?

MIRIAM: No. No. Not at all.

TOMMY: I'm Tommy Reid. (*Offers hand*) And you must be the English woman Rosie said was coming to stay.

MIRIAM: Yes. Miriam Jacobs. How do you do? And this is my daughter, Rachel. Say hello, Rachel.

RACHEL: Hello.

TOMMY: Hello, Rachel, love.

MIRIAM: She pretends to be shy at times.

TOMMY: Don't they all, Mrs Jacobs. You're very beautiful, Rachel, and what's that you're doing? Drawing a beautiful picture? Can I look?

Rachel stares at Tommy suspiciously.

MIRIAM: Show the man your drawing, Rachel.

Tommy looks at the drawing with appropriate gasps.

TOMMY: Are you going to tell me what it is, Rachel?

RACHEL: It's my *daddy*!

TOMMY: Your daddy? And is the beautiful lady with him your mammy?

Rachel nods.

TOMMY: And are you going to draw yourself now?

Rachel looks hesitant and studies Tommy's face.

TOMMY: Why don't you draw Rachel now and then you can show it to Tommy. Will you do that?

Rachel nods and begins drawing intently.

MIRIAM: I'm sorry. Please, won't you sit down? Can I get you something? Tea?

TOMMY: No, thanks, Mrs Jacobs. I'm not stopping. I just called in to say cheerio to Rosie. You see I leave Belfast tomorrow. I'm joining up.

MIRIAM: The Army?

TOMMY: Yes. (*Pause*) Things are bad across the water I hear. In England.

MIRIAM: They're not good. But not as bad as in Europe.

TOMMY: Yes. At least *he* hasn't tried to invade Britain.

MIRIAM: Not yet. But he'll try.

TOMMY: You think so, Mrs Jacobs?

MIRIAM: What's to stop him?

TOMMY: Hopefully, we will. That's . . . that's one of the reasons I'm joining the Army.

MIRIAM: It's brave of you, especially when you don't *have* to. . .

TOMMY: Nothing to do with bravery, Mrs Jacobs. I'm terrified I don't mind telling you . . . but . . . I have my reasons. I fought in Spain with Billy, you see.

MIRIAM: Billy was in Spain?

TOMMY: Yes. Didn't you know?

MIRIAM: No. I didn't.

TOMMY: He had it pretty rough as well. He was captured and imprisoned. Beaten up by the S.S. and those bastards . . . sorry, Mrs Jacobs. . .

MIRIAM: No. You're right. That's what they are.

Pause.

TOMMY: I hope you don't mind me asking, Mrs Jacobs, but are you Jewish?

MIRIAM: Yes. Why?

TOMMY: Please. I didn't mean any offence. It's just Billy and I had a comrade in Spain who was Jewish. Sammy. Sammy Cohen. He was captured the same time as Billy . . . only they. . .

MIRIAM: Killed him?

TOMMY: Yes. (*Pause*) He was a great comrade, Sammy. Little fella. Cockney from London. I think of him often. He had a girl back home in London. He used to write to her every day. Billy and I used to sleg him about it . . . tease him. I remember . . . her name was the same as yours, she was called Miriam, too. That's why I asked about you being Jewish. No offence meant.

Miriam shakes head and smiles.

MIRIAM: None taken.

TOMMY: It must be strange for you — coming here to Belfast, I mean. All this business of Catholics and Protestants.

MIRIAM: It is a little. You are a Catholic?

Tommy laughs.

TOMMY: No. I'm the other sort. I'm a Proddie.

MIRIAM: But you are a friend of Billy's?

TOMMY: Yes. Strange as it may seem, sometimes the two lots, Catholics and Protestants, realize they have more in common than what separates them. We're both working class. We're both socialists . . . which is why Billy and I went to Spain in the first place.

MIRIAM: But he's not going with you this time?

Pause.

TOMMY: No. Not yet anyway. Spain had an effect on Billy.

Enter Rosie.

ROSIE: Would you luk at what the wind blew in!

TOMMY: Hello, Rosie. Are you well?

ROSIE: I'd be a lot better if this bloody war was over, Tommy Reid.

TOMMY: Well, don't you worry, Rosie. Tommy's off to sort out Jerry. I just called to say cheerio, farewell, all the best and that.

ROSIE: When do you leave, son? You've met Miriam and Rachel?

TOMMY: Yes. Yes. We've been having a good aul' yarn. And Rachel's been showing me her picture, haven't you, Rachel?

Rachel smiles.

ROSIE: Are you going to show your drawing to Rosie, Rachel?

Rachel goes to Rosie, pleased. Gets up on Rosie's lap.

ROSIE: Oh, that's a lovely drawing. And who is it?

Rachel giggles.

MIRIAM: Tell Rosie who it is you've drawn, Rachel.

Rachel giggles again and points to Tommy.

RACHEL: Him!

ROSIE: It's Tommy, is it?

TOMMY: Me? Can I look, Rachel?

Rachel nods.

TOMMY: (*Winks at Rachel*) Is that what I look like, Rachel?

ROSIE: It's a very good likeness, don't you think so, Tommy?

TOMMY: The girl's an artist, no doubt about it. I think that drawing deserves a prize.

Tommy gives money to Rachel.

MIRIAM: No. No. Please, you mustn't.

TOMMY: Please. It's nothing.

MIRIAM: Say thank you to Tommy, Rachel.

RACHEL: Thank you, Tommy.

ROSIE: Thank you, *Tommy*? Looks like you've got yourself a girl, Tommy Reid.

TOMMY: It's my looks and charm does it every time, Rosie. Women of all ages find me irresistible!

Tommy pats Rachel on head who runs to her mother.

MIRIAM: Come along, Rachel, we'll leave Rosie and 'Tommy' to talk.

ROSIE: Where are you running off to, Miriam? What Tommy has to say to me I'm sure he can say in front of you. So, when do you leave, Tommy?

TOMMY: The morra mornin, Rosie.

ROSIE: The morra? Are you staying now for a bite of grub?

TOMMY: No. No. I'm not. I have a load of things to do. I just, as I say, popped in briefly. Are you expecting Billy?

Enter Billy.

BILLY: Did somebody mention my name? Hello, everybody. Rachel.

TOMMY: Greetings, Comrade. How's it going?

BILLY: What are you doing here, Reid? I thought you were off dropping bombs on the Nazis.

TOMMY: Tomorrow's the start of my campaign. I called to say all the best.

BILLY: You're really going then?

TOMMY: Aye. I am, Billy. Are you coming with me?

BILLY: You must be bloody joking. I've told you what my feelings are on that score.

TOMMY: Aye, well. . .

BILLY: And you wouldn't be going either only you've taken to seeing visions. . .

TOMMY: It's not the only reason, Billy, and you know it. It's part of the same fight we fought in Spain.

BILLY: Don't talk to me about fighting and war, Tommy Reid. I know all about them. I know too bloody much about them.

RACHEL: Mummy, what's a war?

MIRIAM: Come along, Rachel. We'll go upstairs and you can finish your drawing.

RACHEL: I don't want to go upstairs.

MIRIAM: Rachel?

ROSIE: Will you come with me, Rachel? That's a good girl. Rosie has a surprise for you.

Rosie takes Rachel's hand and goes to leave. She stops by Tommy.

ROSIE: Say 'bye-'bye, to Tommy. Have you a kiss for him?

Tommy bends down to kiss Rachel.

TOMMY: 'Bye-'bye, Rachel. See you soon.

ROSIE: He better, Rachel, better in' he? Otherwise he'll be in severe trouble with Rosie and Rachel. (*To Tommy*) Look after yourself son. Drop us a wee note if you get the chance. You'll be in my prayers.

TOMMY: Thanks, Rosie. You take care of yourself, too. And tell Jimmy I was asking for him.

ROSIE: I will, son. All the best. God Bless. (*She hugs Tommy*) Right, Rachel, that surprise, c'mon to we see.

Rosie exits with Rachel.
Pause.
Tommy looks from Miriam to Billy.

TOMMY: Aye . . . right . . . well . . . I better be off. Nice meeting you, Mrs Jacobs. That's a lovely wee girl you have there.

MIRIAM: Thank you, Tommy. It's been nice talking to you. And . . . Good Luck!

TOMMY: Thanks. (*To Billy*) Alright, then, Billy, I'll be seeing you.

BILLY: Aye. Be seeing you.

TOMMY: I'll drop you a line.

BILLY: Whatever you like yourself.

TOMMY: All the best then.

Tommy goes to exit.

BILLY: Tommy?

TOMMY: Yes, Comrade?

Pause.

BILLY: Watch your step, eh?

TOMMY: You too, Billy. You too.

Tommy smiles, nods and exits.
Silence.
Miriam watches Billy who catches her eye but looks away.
Off-stage, we hear voices.

TOMMY: Oh, Mr Robinson. Glad to catch you. Just called to say cheerio. I leave the morra.

JIMMY: Oh, you do, do you? Well, when you're over there, Tommy Reid, tell your Orange friend, Mr Winston Churchill, him of the Orange card trick, that we're not all like you . . . some of us are Irish and neutral, and Irish and neutral we're going to stay!

TOMMY: Aye, I'll tell him. Goodbye, Mr Robinson.

Pause.
Enter Jimmy.

JIMMY: Protestants! More bloody English than the English themselves!

Exchange of looks between Jimmy, Billy and Miriam.
Slow fade.

5 | SCENE

Robinson kitchen. Dinner table. Dinner completed — at tea and biscuits stage. Pause.

ROSIE: Does anybody want more tea? Miriam?

MIRIAM: No, thank you.

RACHEL: May I leave the table, Mummy?

ROSIE: Of course you can, love. You run off and play if you wish.

Rachel gets down from table and exits.
Miriam starts clearing table.

ROSIE: Leave those, Miriam. Sit down and rest yourself there a bit. We can sort them out afterwards.

Pause.

MIRIAM: Mr Robinson. . .

ROSIE: Call him, Jimmy, Miriam. Everybody round here is known by their handle.

Miriam smiles at Rosie but she is tense.

MIRIAM: Do you mind if I ask you a question?

ROSIE: Jimmy, the woman's talking to you. Could you put down that bloody newspaper for a second?

Jimmy folds paper and looks towards Miriam.

MIRIAM: Mr Robinson — Jimmy — why are you so against fighting the Germans? The Nazis?

JIMMY: It's England's war. Not Ireland's.

MIRIAM: I don't understand . . . isn't it a war against Fascism?

JIMMY: That's as maybe. But it's England has declared war on Germany. Ireland hasn't. It's not our war. It has nothing to do with us.

MIRIAM: Would you say the same if Hitler attacked Ireland?

JIMMY: But he hasn't.

BILLY: Not yet, Da. Not yet.

JIMMY: And why would Hitler attack Ireland?

BILLY: You might ask the same of Poland or Czechoslovakia or any of the other countries in Europe.

JIMMY: This isn't Europe. This is Ireland. Besides our relationship with Germany has always been friendly. Germany in the past has been a friend to Ireland . . . an ally . . . look no further than the aid given to Roger Casement.

MIRIAM: Perhaps Ireland needs to examine more closely who its friends are, Mr Robinson?

JIMMY: Well, it hasn't been England, Mrs Jacobs, it hasn't been England! England has been the oppressor of Ireland for centuries in case you didn't know. Let her give us freedom before she starts preaching at us as to who our friends should be.

MIRIAM: I wasn't preaching, Mr Robinson. And though I was born in England, I'm not exactly English now, am I?

JIMMY: Aren't you?

ROSIE: I think that's enough, Jimmy. May I remind you that Miriam is a guest in this house. And she's here because of Mr Hitler and his antics.

JIMMY: And may I remind you, Rosie, and Mrs Jacobs, that

being the case, it's Ireland is giving her refuge. You don't attack those who've made you welcome.

MIRIAM: I'm sorry, Mr Robinson. I wasn't attacking you or Ireland. And I'm grateful to be here, to have your hospitality, but if you don't want me. . .

ROSIE: Jimmy's not saying that. Sure you're not, Jimmy. The woman was only asking you a question Jimmy, she didn't ask for a lecture on Irish history.

JIMMY: Look here, Mrs Jacobs. I'm sorry for you. I'm sorry you had to be evacuated from your home. . .

MIRIAM: Jews are used to that, Mr Robinson. I was born in England because my parents were fleeing persecution in Europe. Oppression is not new to us. You say Ireland has been oppressed by England for centuries. We Jews have been oppressed in every country we've ever been in for two thousand years, Mr Robinson. Two thousand years!

JIMMY: I don't know anything about that, but what I do know. . .

BILLY: Maybe it's time you found out about it, Da, instead of thinking about Ireland all the bloody time.

JIMMY: And what's wrong with thinking about Ireland? What's wrong with fighting for Ireland? Christ, somebody has to, we can't all be running off and fighting or not fighting wars in other countries all the time. If people sorted out their own house and put it in order we wouldn't have half the problems we have. Jesus, you're one to talk, Billy. You went to Spain to fight *Fascism* and look what happened to you.

ROSIE: That's enough, Jimmy. We've been through all that before. Leave our Billy and Spain out of this.

BILLY: No. No, Ma. It's alright. What were you going to say, Da? What about me and Spain and fighting *Fascism*?

MIRIAM: Billy, please. I'm sorry Rosie. I didn't mean to start. . .

BILLY: It's alright, Miriam. You haven't started anything. Nothing that wouldn't have started at some point any road. You want to pick at the sore of Spain, Da. You go ahead, but you listen to me. Yeh, I 'ran' as you would put it, Da. I left the ranks — after seeing something you have no idea about.

JIMMY: I have plenty of ideas, don't you kid yourself.

BILLY: Aye, so you have. And all of them, bloody cock-eyed and bigoted. You think because you fought in nineteen bloody sixteen and in the Civil War you have the right to pronounce on everything — everything you know nothing about.

JIMMY: I know what I have to know. I know what a 'coward' is, Billy. . .

BILLY: Alright, Da . . . and you think I was a coward. . .

MIRIAM: Billy. . .

BILLY: Aye. Well, maybe I was and maybe I wasn't. But let me tell you, Da, there was nothing cowardly about the wee man that I took with me . . . the wee man who saw what I saw and went 'insane' because of it . . . the wee man who was incapable of coping with any of it anymore . . . but do you want to know what happened to him when we were caught, Da? Do you? He wasn't imprisoned like I was. . . I was 'lucky' . . . no, wee Sammy Cohen, *Jewish* Sammy Cohen, was shot on the spot, that's what happened to him, Da. And you wanna know why? Why he was executed on the spot and I wasn't? — for we were both Republicans, Da, we were both members of the International Brigade — only, he was a Jew, Da. Sammy Cohen was Jewish . . . and when those S.S. bastards realized, they couldn't wait to fill him full of lead. They couldn't wait to murder another Jew. Me? I was just another undesirable alien to them, another revolutionary socialist from a foreign country. I was just a follower of James Connolly fighting on the losing side again, just like you were Da. But Sammy Cohen was not just an Internationalist but also a Jew! They murdered him. They imprisoned me. And your German friends, Da, are doing the same right now — murdering Jews for being Jews. Miriam's right, Ireland needs to look again at who she thinks her friends are. You need to think, Da, long and hard who your friends are!

Pause.

JIMMY: I obviously haven't got many in this house. I suppose you'll be appearing in a British Army uniform the next time I see you . . . running off to join your English-loving friend, your Protestant comrade, Tommy Reid . . . or maybe you won't . . . maybe you haven't got the guts!

Billy jumps up angry and grim-faced.
Jimmy slowly rises, looks at Billy with disdain and exits.
Silence.

MIRIAM: Rosie. . .

ROSIE: Don't you **apologize**, Miriam, don't you dare. All this has been coming for a long time. . . It's been a long time in the coming . . . the trigger's been cocked for manys a day now. . .

MIRIAM: Billy . . . I'm sorry. . .

BILLY: It's nothing. I think I'll go for a bit of a dander, Ma. Will you be alright?

ROSIE: Me? And why wouldn't I? Because your father raises his voice and starts a row? It's nothing new to Rosie Magee. I've heard it all before, son, the rantings and ravings of Ireland's hero. No, away on with you. The dander and fresh air'll do you good.

MIRIAM: Can I come with you, Billy?

ROSIE: Good idea. Away the two of yiz go. Your Da'll be heading for McGlinchey's. . .

ROSIE: Now, where's that wee beauty of a Rachel. Her and me'll have a civilized chat about the wonders of childhood. Go on. Away with yiz.

MIRIAM: Are you sure, Rosie? You don't mind watching Rachel?

ROSIE: Get! Sure, I'll be glad of the sanity of innocence.

Miriam hugs Rosie.
Miriam and Billy exit.
Silence.
Enter Rachel.

RACHEL: Rosie! Rosie! Look what Billy gave me.

ROSIE: C'mere til I see. C'mon and sit up on Rosie's knee and tell me all. Tell me all.

Blackout.

SCENE 6

Falls Park. Billy and Miriam sitting on bench.

MIRIAM: I think maybe I should leave, Billy. Go away. Go back to England.

BILLY: Why?

MIRIAM: Why? It seems clear to me your father doesn't want me here.

BILLY: You'll break my Ma's heart if you leave now. She's taken to you and little Rachel and if my Ma takes to somebody, that's it. It's the same with Tommy.

MIRIAM: I liked Tommy.

BILLY: He's one of the best. There's not many in this town like him.

MIRIAM: But your father, Billy. . .

BILLY: My Da's bark is worse than his bite. You should pay no attention to him. I should pay no attention to his rantin' and ravin's.

MIRIAM: I'm sorry for what happened, Billy. It was my fault for asking him about Ireland and Germany.

BILLY: Don't talk nonsense. Why shouldn't you ask him what you asked? It was a valid question.

MIRIAM: All the same, he's right. I am a guest in his house.

BILLY: Aye. And he wasn't exactly the epitome of Irish hospitality, now was he! No, you see, Miriam, my Da's a very bitter man. He feels betrayed and rightly so. And betrayal can make monsters of people. It can make them narrow-minded, bigoted and obsessive. And my Da is all of those.

MIRIAM: But why, Billy?

BILLY: Why? It's a long story, Miriam. Very long.

MIRIAM: I'd like to know. Tell me. I need to know if I'm to try to understand.

BILLY: I wish he'd try to understand. Perhaps he does deep down, but the old obsessions blinker him.

MIRIAM: Obsessions?

BILLY: My father, Miriam, as you will have gathered, fought in 1916, in the Easter Rising. He was a member of Pearse's Volunteers. He believed he was fighting for the freedom of Ireland and he was. Then the Civil War broke out between those who accepted the Treaty with the English and Partition and those who didn't. My Da didn't. Like De Valera didn't. They fought and killed and were killed by those who'd been their comrades in the War of Independence against the English. But they lost. Like Tommy and I lost in Spain. The cause was right and just, but it lost. History seems to be like that, Miriam, the just causes always lose. It's like there's somethin' in the atmosphere that always means that evil wins out. Anyway . . . civil wars are bitter-making episodes especially if you believe, like my Da, that your side was right and with your defeat, Right has been defeated. It's a bitter pill to swallow, and I know my Da to this day doesn't comprehend why it happened, which is why he flails about having a go at anything which doesn't fit into the old obsession . . . the old dream, the old ideal, which has become an obsession. It's the obsession of my Da. It's the obsession of our Mr Eamonn De Valera — political freedom and independence for Ireland. It's that sore of a partitioned Ireland which festers and makes Ireland neutral today. It's that gaping wound made by England that causes people like De Valera and my Da to be so obsessed with what had been their youthful dream that they are incapable of seeing beyond their nationalistic noses.

MIRIAM: Do you mean, if Ireland were free . . . if there was no partition . . . a United Ireland wouldn't remain neutral in the face of Hitler?

BILLY: Who knows, Miriam? Who knows? The fact is Ireland isn't free. The country's divided. And as it stands she is neutral.

Pause.

MIRIAM: Do *you* agree with Ireland's neutrality?

BILLY: Me? I neither agree with it nor disagree. I can understand, I think, why it is. I can even understand why my Da sees England's enemy as Ireland's friend. . . England does have a long history of oppressing Ireland, Miriam . . . almost within living memory, there was the Famine or Starvation of 1845, when a policy of near genocide was implemented against the Irish, when the population was halved, when the Irish people were dispersed to the four corners of the earth. The Irish diaspora, you might call it. The race memory of such things, Miriam, makes people happily revengeful when they witness the traditional enemy getting a dose of their own punishment. That's why I can understand people like my father, Miriam.

MIRIAM: But you don't agree with him? I just heard you rowing with him. And *you* don't have his 'obsession', as you call it, you can't have. You went and fought in Spain. You and **Tommy fought Fascism in Spain!**

BILLY: And lost Miriam. And lost.

MIRIAM: Yes. But Fascism hasn't gone away, Billy. It's spread. It's not just in Spain, it's riddled throughout Europe.

BILLY: *You're telling me?*

MIRIAM: I'm sorry, Billy. I know you know but I . . . I can't understand. . .

BILLY: Why I haven't gone off with Tommy to join the British **Army and fight Fascism in Europe?**

MIRIAM: Well, yes. It's the same fight. It's the same war you fought in Spain. It's the same cause. . .

BILLY: And what cause is that, Miriam?

MIRIAM: The cause of freedom. . .

BILLY: Freedom? And you think fighting wars brings freedom?

MIRIAM: What else are we to do, Billy, but fight evil?

BILLY: Evil? Now there's a word takes some defining!

MIRIAM: Doesn't Hitler and Fascism and the Nazis fit any such definition? Doesn't killing Jews because they are Jews fit such a definition? You said yourself, you saw it in Spain with Sammy, Sammy Cohen — murdered for being a Jew. What about all the Sammy Cohens being butchered now in Europe, Billy? What about them? Don't they deserve to be fought for? Don't they have a right to live? Alright, maybe war doesn't bring freedom. It didn't in Spain — you know that, you were there. But Jews in Europe. Jews like me, Billy, we are not fighting for freedom . . . we're trying to stay alive . . . only trying to survive! *Survive*, Billy! Survive!

Miriam begins to cry. Billy goes to her, she turns to sob on his shoulder.

MIRIAM: Tell me what happened to you in Spain, Billy. Please tell me. Please!

Miriam looks into Billy's face. Tears streaming down her face.
Hold. Blackout.

7 SCENE

Robinson kitchen. Rosie sitting, darning. Enter Billy and Miriam.

ROSIE: Ah, youse are back. I put little Rachel to bed, Miriam.

MIRIAM: Thank you, Rosie. I'm sorry we were so long.

ROSIE: She was dead beat, the child, but I enjoyed her company while she lasted. I said you'd look in on her when you got back, but I'd think she's probably fast asleep by now.

BILLY: Where's my Da?

ROSIE: He's not back. Sure they haven't closed yet, have they?

BILLY: Well, I think I'll go on to bed. I have work in the morning.

ROSIE: Do you want anything, Billy? Cup of tea or anything?

BILLY: No, thanks, Ma. I'll go on. Goodnight. (*Pause*) Goodnight, Miriam.

Moment between Billy and Miriam.

MIRIAM: Goodnight, Billy.

ROSIE: Goodnight, son. God Bless. See you in the morning, God willin'.

BILLY: Goodnight.

Billy exits.

ROSIE: You'll have a wee cup of tea with me, won't you, Miriam?

MIRIAM: I'd love one, Rosie. Can I do anything?

ROSIE: Not at all. Sure there's nothing to do. (*Pause*) Enjoy your dander then?

MIRIAM: Sorry?

ROSIE: Your dander . . . your walk out with Billy?

MIRIAM: Yes . . . yes, we went up as far as the park.

Pause.

ROSIE: You seem preoccupied, Miriam. Want to talk about it?

MIRIAM: I'm sorry, Rosie. I'm just going over some of the things Billy said.

ROSIE: Hmmm. Hmmm!

Pause.

MIRIAM: He told me about Spain, Rosie. And what happened.

ROSIE: He did?

MIRIAM: Your son's a very brave and good man, Rosie.

ROSIE: There's worse.

MIRIAM: He told me about the terrible atrocities committed on both sides and about the execution of priests and nuns and why he . . . 'left' the Republican side and how he and his comrade, Sammy Cohen, were captured by the S.S. And how he was beaten and tortured in prison.

ROSIE: He had it rough alright, did our Billy. That war in Spain must have been like visitin' hell. But he's better now than he was. He was in an awful state when he first came home. I think it was the mental anguish of what he had witnessed rather than any physical treatment the Fascists had meted out to him personally.

MIRIAM: Yes. He told me.

ROSIE: But thank God my prayers were answered and he was released.

MIRIAM: In a prisoner exchange, he told me.

ROSIE: Aye. (*Pause*) Did he tell you about Tommy Reid?

MIRIAM: What about Tommy?

ROSIE: Poor Tommy. He suffered too. Not in the way Billy did, but sufferin' is sufferin'. Tommy had met a woman in Spain . . . an Englishwoman . . . she was an artist, I believe . . . very posh but she was there, fighting for the Republicans. Anyway, Tommy had fallen in love with this Englishwoman but the poor girl was killed during the fighting. Tommy was devastated. He was, according to Billy, very deeply in love with her. Billy used to sleg him about it when they were first in Spain but then. . .

MIRIAM: No, I didn't know that. He didn't say. There were so many other things we talked about. Like why Ireland is neutral in this war with Germany. I think I understand why a bit better than I did. Rosie, I'm sorry I asked Jimmy. . .

ROSIE: Why should you be sorry for asking a question? Catch yourself on, girl, there's nothing to be sorry about. Jimmy's. . .

MIRIAM: All the same, I think it would be better if I left. I don't want to leave. I like it here with you, Rosie, and I know Rachel has grown especially fond of you. . .

ROSIE: And I of both of you. So what's the problem? Listen here, Miriam Jacobs, there's no question of you leaving. Where would you go . . . back to England? Maybe to be bombed by Mr Hitler? No. I won't hear of it. I'd never forgive myself if something did happen to ye or wee Rachel.

MIRIAM: Billy said you'd object.

ROSIE: And he was right. Now let's hear nothing more about it. You're stopping and that's that. I'll take care of Jimmy Robinson, have no fear on that score. He's full of lip is Jimmy. Doesn't mean half of what he says any road.

MIRIAM: Billy said that too.

ROSIE: There you are then. Two independent opinions. Great minds think alike, and don't you dare say the rest of it, Miriam Jacobs.

MIRIAM: You're very kind, Rosie. I can see who Billy takes after.

ROSIE: Oh, he has his father in him as well. They're not unalike in many ways. And the world has done similar things to both of them.

MIRIAM: What do you mean?

ROSIE: Oh, they're both shattered men living with shattered dreams. Men are proud beings, Miriam. They don't like having weaknesses and to have shattered dreams they feel is a weakness, but they forget we know them from birth to death. And that we have dreams too. Big dreams and little dreams that are shattered daily but we still dream. The likes of Jimmy and our Billy haven't learnt yet how to dream again. It may be too late for Jimmy but there's still time for our Billy. . .

Off-stage we hear a door banging and the voice of Jimmy singing Rebel song.
Enter Jimmy. He is very drunk. Says nothing. Sways to and fro, then collapses onto sofa, oblivious.
Hold. Blackout.

8 SCENE

Robinson home. Morning time. Miriam is getting washed in scullery dressed only in slip.
Enter Billy in trousers, no shirt. He heads for kitchen, realizes Miriam is there, walks back into kitchen embarrassed.

BILLY: I'm sorry. I didn't realize there was anyone. . .

MIRIAM: It's alright, Billy. I'm finished. Thank you.

Miriam emerges from scullery drying face with towel.

MIRIAM: Sorry. I'm keeping you back. You have work to go to. It's just I couldn't sleep . . . thought I'd be done before anyone. . .

Miriam stops. Realizing Billy is watching her. Moment.

BILLY: Well, I better get a move on or I'll be late for that job of work I have to go to.

Billy goes into scullery to wash. Miriam puts on dress. As Billy re-enters kitchen, Miriam adjusting stocking. Billy stops again, looks. Miriam catches his eye. Looks at Billy without shirt. Moment. Billy puts on shirt. Enter Jimmy looking the worse for wear. Heads straight for scullery.

BILLY: Good morning, Da. Good night?

MIRIAM: Good morning, Mr Robinson.

Jimmy says nothing but groans to himself. Billy and Miriam silently laugh to each other.

BILLY: (*Looking at clock*) Jesus, is that the time? I am late and I wasn't kicking the gong around. . .

Billy nods again in direction of scullery. Miriam smiles. Billy goes to exit, turns.

BILLY: You'll be here tonight then?

MIRIAM: Yes.

BILLY: See you then.

Enter Rosie, almost collides with Billy.

ROSIE: Where are you off to?

BILLY: Work, Ma. Work!

ROSIE: Without your breakfast again? Sure that's no way to be going out of a morning.

BILLY: Bye, Ma. (*Kisses her on cheek and exits*)

MIRIAM: Good morning, Rosie.

ROSIE: Good morning, love. You're up early this morning.

MIRIAM: Couldn't sleep.

ROSIE: Aye. Probably the noise of that Jimmy fella snoring. Did you hear the rattles of him? It would've woken the dead. Kept me awake half the bloody night!

Jimmy enters kitchen from scullery.

ROSIE: And I suppose you're going without any breakfast as well?

Jimmy ignores her though he probably doesn't hear. Puts on work boots and jacket and exits.

ROSIE: Didya ever see anything like it, the cut of him? Patrick Pearse with a hangover.

Miriam laughs. Enter Rachel.

MIRIAM: Rachel! I thought you were still asleep, sweetheart.

Rachel shakes her head, rubs her eyes and yawns.

ROSIE: Good morning, little one. You're just in time. Your mammy and I and you will have a nice breakfast together. And then I think we three will take a wee trip into town. You never know what we might come back with. A couple of kilties!

Rosie kisses Rachel and goes into scullery.

RACHEL: What's a kiltie, mummy?

MIRIAM: I don't know, Rachel. You'll have to get Rosie to explain over breakfast. Now, would you like to run upstairs and bring down your clothes, and then you can get washed and dressed. We'll have breakfast with Rosie and then go into town.

Miriam kisses and hugs Rachel who runs off — exits. Miriam goes into scullery.

MIRIAM: Is there anything I can do, Rosie?

ROSIE: Aye. Set the table there, Miriam. You should find everything you need in that cupboard.

Miriam returns from scullery with cups etc. Sets table.

ROSIE: (*From scullery*) You know, Miriam, having that child of yours in the house is like a tonic to me. It makes me realize what a strain it's been living with those two shattered dreams of men I have.

Rosie in doorway.

ROSIE: And you are staying, aren't you, Miriam?

Pause.

MIRIAM: I'd like to.

ROSIE: That's settled then. (*Turns back into scullery*) Billy looked in fine fettle this morning. Maybe he's beginning to 'dream' again.

Miriam smiles, then matter of factly

MIRIAM: Yes. Maybe he is. (*To herself*) Maybe he is.

Hold on Miriam smiling to herself. Rosie looks out from scullery but unseen by Miriam.
Blackout.

9 | SCENE

Robinson kitchen, evening. Miriam in new dress, preening herself in mirror. Silence. Enter Billy.

BILLY: Hello. (*Looks around*) Have they all left you holding the fort again on your own?

MIRIAM: Your mother has gone across to see a friend. She took Rachel with her, or Rachel took her, I'm not sure which.

Billy laughs, removes work boots etc.

BILLY: My Ma won't object to that. (*Pause*) You decided to stay then?

MIRIAM: Yes.

Pause.

BILLY: Good. I'm glad. (*Pause*) Well, I'll just go and have a bit of a wash.

Billy turns but stops in scullery doorway. Looks back at Miriam.

BILLY: I like your dress.

MIRIAM: Thank you. It's new. Your mother insisted I buy it. We were in town today.

BILLY: Nothing could make my Ma happier than a jaunt round the town with another woman. I suppose youse were in every shop in town.

MIRIAM: Probably. Yes. She did seem to be enjoying herself. I did, too.

BILLY: Well, you're certainly looking. . .

Billy embarrassed. Retreats to scullery. Miriam turns to glance at herself in mirror again. Billy appears back in doorway.

BILLY: Miriam?

MIRIAM: Yes, Billy?

BILLY: I don't suppose you'd fancy. . .

MIRIAM: What?

BILLY: I don't suppose you'd fancy going out for a fish supper, would you? Jesus, what an invite, eh?

MIRIAM: I'd like to, Billy, but what about your mother and Rachel? Your mother'll be back soon to make the dinner.

Pause.

BILLY: We could leave them a wee note. Tell them where we are. My Ma won't mind, and we won't be long.

MIRIAM: Alright. If you're sure. . .

Billy disappears hurriedly into scullery.

BILLY: I won't be a second in getting ready.

Miriam turns and looks in mirror, smiles pleased.
Music and sound.
Cross-fade to café.
Billy and Miriam. Miriam finishing off fish and chips.
Lays down knife and fork. Wipes mouth. Billy watches.

MIRIAM: I haven't enjoyed fish and chips so much in a caff for I don't know how long.

BILLY: Aye. It takes the Italians to come to Belfast to make good fish and chips.

MIRIAM: What? Is this place owned by Italians?

BILLY: Aye. They speak Italian too with a Belfast accent.

Miriam laughs.

BILLY: Would you like something else? Italian ice-cream?

MIRIAM: No thanks. That was lovely.

BILLY: Cup of tea? Coffee? They do coffee.

MIRIAM: No. Nothing thanks. I'm fine. You must let me pay for this, Billy.

BILLY: No chance!

MIRIAM: I'd like to.

BILLY: Another time maybe.

MIRIAM: Alright. Next time it's my treat.

Pause.

BILLY: So, tell me about you, Miriam? You know a brave bit about me as it is.

MIRIAM: Well, I'm Jewish as you know. My parents were from Roumania. They're both dead.

Pause.

BILLY: I'm sorry, Miriam.

MIRIAM: (*Shrugs*) It happens to us all, Billy. I was born in Manchester. And lived there all my life until . . . until now. . .

BILLY: Your husband?

MIRIAM: My husband?

BILLY: I'm sorry, Miriam. It's none of my business. . .

MIRIAM: But you're curious. You'd like to know.

BILLY: No . . . well. . .

MIRIAM: It's alright, Billy. I don't mind talking about it. I've told your mother . . . she obviously hasn't said. . .

BILLY: She hasn't said a thing to me.

Pause.

MIRIAM: My husband's in the Air Force, Billy. The British Air Force.

BILLY: Is he . . . Jewish?

MIRIAM: Yes. (*Pause*) He's also missing, Billy. I don't know where he is. And neither does the Air Force. 'Missing in action' is what they call it, I think.

BILLY: I'm sorry. (*Pause*) How. . .

MIRIAM: . . . long has it been? Six months.

BILLY: And nothing? No news at all?

MIRIAM: No. Nothing. His plane went missing on a mission. They presume he was shot down, but there's no evidence to suggest exactly what happened. (*Pause*) Sometimes I dream that he's still up there . . . flying about . . . lost among the clouds. . .

BILLY: Does wee Rachel. . .?

MIRIAM: (*Shakes head*) She knows her daddy has gone to war but nothing else. She asks. Like the other day, she asked when was he coming to live with us in Rosie's house. She also asked . . . what's a war, Mummy?

BILLY: And how do you explain to a child that it's a man-made hell which no vision of hell can describe?

Silence. Billy seems to go off into trance.

MIRIAM: Billy?

BILLY: Hmmm. . .

MIRIAM: What is it? What are you thinking?

Billy comes back, stares at Miriam.

BILLY: I'm thinking what an eejit I've been, what a selfish get. . .

MIRIAM: But why? *Why?*

BILLY: Because I lectured you the other night about wars and fighting and felt sorry for myself and I never thought to ask myself once — I never thought to ask you — *why* it was *you* were evacuated or why it was you didn't have a husband. Jesus, why didn't I realize? Why didn't I know? And I lecture my Da about selfishness and narrow vision, when you . . . you. . .

MIRIAM: But how could you know, Billy? How could you. . .?

BILLY: How could I hear you say that it's the same war against Fascism and not twig on? How could I hear you say that Jews are fighting to survive in Europe and not realize that you had a husband? A Jew, a Jew like Sammy Cohen in Spain. You mentioned Sammy. I remember. Jesus, how could I be such a fool? Such a bloody damned fool. . . (*Pause*) Miriam. . . I am sorry. . .

Miriam gets up, kisses him lightly on lips.
They stare at each other.
Then embrace passionately. Blackout.

2 Act

1 SCENE

Three months later. In a public house. Billy and Miriam with Tommy who is home on leave. Tommy brings over drinks.

TOMMY: Well, now, good to see you both. All the best.

   Drinks business.

BILLY AND MIRIAM: All the best, Tommy.

TOMMY: Aaaaah! I've been looking forward to that. A good drop of creamy Liffey water. So what's the crack? How have things been in Belfast town? You're both looking very well! (*Tommy winks at Miriam*)

BILLY: You're not looking bad yourself, Tommy Reid. The British Army must be looking after you well.

TOMMY: Oh aye, very well, Billy. They haven't got me killed yet so I suppose they must be. How's your mother?

BILLY: The best. She hasn't been in such good form for years. Having Miriam's wee Rachel around all the time has taken years off her.

MIRIAM: They're like a double act, Tommy. You never see one but you see the other.

TOMMY: That's great. She's a beautiful wee girl, that Rachel.

BILLY: Takes after her mother, Tommy.

TOMMY: Very true, William. Very true.

MIRIAM: Flattery will get you boys anywhere.

    Laughter.

TOMMY: And what about your father, Billy? How's Jimmy?

BILLY: Still waging war against Churchill along with the help of Eamonn De Valera.

TOMMY: No change on that front then, eh?

BILLY: Did you expect any, Tommy? If anything he's got worse.

MIRIAM: Billy! That's not entirely true now.

BILLY: Oh, he keeps a button on his lip when Miriam and the child are around but that's more to do with the threatening presence of my Ma than any change of heart.

TOMMY: A great woman Rosie. I think of your mother often when I'm away. Keeps the heart up at times.

BILLY: You'll call to see her? She'll be furious if you don't.

TOMMY: I'll look in on her, but I haven't a great deal of time.

MIRIAM: When are you due back, Tommy?

TOMMY: The day after the morra. I arise and go to meet Jerry again.

BILLY: And how is. . . ?

TOMMY: It has its moments, Billy. It has its moments. . . But Christ, I'm on leave, man. I'm not here to. . . Has this fella been looking after you alright, Miriam? For if he hasn't. . .

BILLY: More like she's been looking after me.

TOMMY: Signs on you too, Billy Robinson. You know, I wouldn't have believed it, but since I left your face has changed.

BILLY: Thanks, Tommy. What the hell are you. . .

TOMMY: No. I mean your whole expression, everything about you has been transformed, and that's no exaggeration. You nearly look human again. . .

They feint boxing.

TOMMY: And I assume you are responsible, Miriam?

MIRIAM: Nothing to do with me, Tommy.

Miriam and Billy exchange warm look.

BILLY: Nah, you're right, Tommy. I have changed. In fact there's been quite a few changes all in all.

TOMMY: I can see that.

BILLY: The biggest one being . . . I've made a decision. . . Miriam doesn't know anything about this yet. . .

MIRIAM: What are you talking about, Billy?

Pause.

BILLY: I'm joining up.

TOMMY: Are you serious, Billy?

MIRIAM: You never said anything, Billy. When did you. . .

BILLY: It can't surprise you, Miriam, after the talks we've had.

MIRIAM: No, but. . .

TOMMY: Ho! Ho! Jerry'd better look out now that Robinson's joining the ranks. Have you told your Da yet?

BILLY: No. Not yet. This is the first I've said. . .

TOMMY: Christ, I'd love to be there to see his face when you do. What a picture that'll make!

MIRIAM: Will you excuse me, please?

BILLY: Miriam? Where are you going?

Miriam leaves without answering.

BILLY: Miriam?

Billy looks at Tommy anxiously.

BILLY: Here, Tommy, get another drink in. I'll be back in a minute. I don't know what. . .

TOMMY: Go ahead, Billy. Go ahead. I'll be here.

Exit Billy. Cross-fade to Miriam, who has been crying. Enter Billy.

BILLY: Miriam?

Miriam doesn't turn, but hurriedly puts away hankie.

BILLY: Miriam? Why did you leave?

Billy approaches her and turns her round. He sees that she has been crying.

BILLY: Miriam, what are you crying for, love? I thought you'd be pleased. I thought you wanted me to. . .

MIRIAM: Join the British Army and get yourself killed? Is that what you thought, Billy Robinson, is it?

BILLY: Nobody's going off to get themselves killed, Miriam. But after our talks, you said . . . you told me it's the same fight I fought in Spain and you were right, Miriam. If anything it's more important we fight Fascism now than then.

MIRIAM: It's important to fight it at any time, Billy.

BILLY: Well, then? What's the problem? Why are you objecting to my doing so now?

MIRIAM: I'm not, Billy. I'm not. But I don't want you to do it now simply because of me . . . because of what I said. . .

BILLY: I don't deny, you and what we've talked about have influenced my thinking, Miriam, but I don't think they're the only reasons for my decision. I went to Spain before I'd ever met you.

MIRIAM: And you came back a shattered man, Billy. Don't you think maybe you've done enough fighting? You suffered terribly in Spain, Billy . . . you've recovered in part . . . I don't want you to suffer again.

Miriam turns away. Pause. Billy walks round to face her.

BILLY: Miriam! I am what I am now in no small measure because of you. . .

MIRIAM: And can't you see, Billy, that's just it. I don't want you to go out of gratitude to me.

BILLY: But I am grateful to you, Miriam. I shall be for always . . . but I'm not joining the British Army to go and fight Nazis because of that. I'm going for the same reason as Tommy went. The same reason as he and I first went to Spain.

MIRIAM: But you said Tommy only joined the Army because of his 'visions'. You mocked him for it. You scorned him. You said he was only doing it because of his 'dead love'.

BILLY: Yes, I did, Miriam. And maybe he did. I don't know. And if it was his only motivation, though I don't believe it was, can it not be said he was right . . . can it not be said that there is a beauty to it. . .? Can it not be said that to fight for love of someone is the *only* real motivation worth having. To fight only for an ideology — an ideal, an abstraction, call it freedom, democracy, socialism, whatever you like — is but part of the argument and the cold part at that. The Nazis, Miriam, are fighting for an ideology. Be that they were fighting out of love — for love — there would not be a war on. *I love you, Miriam.* And I know of no greater motive or reason for leaving you to go and fight Fascism. If love has any power in it, it is only with love that we will win. That we will defeat those without love. That we will crush those motivated by hate. (*Pause*) I love you, Miriam.

Pause.

MIRIAM: I'm frightened, Billy. Frightened. I've lost a husband already. I don't want to lose a lover as well. I don't want to lose you. I love you, Billy.

Embrace.
Cross-fade back to bar. Tommy sitting drinking. Enter Jimmy with glass in hand, obviously drunk.

JIMMY: Reid? Reid? Is it you?

TOMMY: Hello, Mr Robinson. How are you doing?

Jimmy aggressively into Tommy's face.

JIMMY: I thought it was. And I was right. I says to myself, yon looks like Orange Lodge features. Yon looks like yon wee Protestant skitter from the Shankill Road, says I to myself. And I was right so I was . . . I was right. Yon's a British soldier says I. Yon's the Sweeney Todd 'comrade' of our yellow-bellied Billy who both pretended to be Republicans and went to Spain and now look at them. Now look at them!

TOMMY: You're in quare form I see, Jimmy. . .

JIMMY: Mr Robinson to you, son. *Mr Robinson!* A real Republican! A true Republican! Did you know that I was in the Post Office along with Patrick Pearse? Did you know that, did you? Well you shoulda fuckin' well known it, you wee slabberin' English-lovin' Protestant get that you are. . .

TOMMY: All the best, Mr Robinson. Be seeing you. Watch your step.

JIMMY: Watch my step? I don't need the likes of you to tell me to watch my step. Here . . . here . . . where do you think you're going? I haven't finished talking to you yet. I haven't finished with you, not by a long chalk. Here. Here. Come back here. Come back . . . you traitorous bigoted wee shitehawk. Come back, I said. Come. . .

Jimmy stumbles over table. Glasses go crashing. Jimmy falls to floor. Enter Billy and Miriam to witness descent. Hold.
Blackout.

SCENE | 2

Robinson home.
Miriam, alone. Reading letter from Billy.
Spot on Billy in British Army Uniform. Separate.

As Miriam reads letter, it is the voice of Billy we hear.

BILLY: Dearest Miriam, you know, writing that 'dearest Miriam' reminds me of Sammy in Spain. Sammy Cohen. I told you how he used to write to his girl, Miriam, in London and how Tommy and I used to sleg him to death. Isn't it strange that I should now be writing to *my* Miriam — my love. The coincidence of it pleases me, for I feel in part that I am writing it for Sammy as well as myself. And you know, Miriam, now that I'm here, I feel I'm here for Sammy as much as for anything else. I remember how it surprised Tommy and me, the kind of people we found in Spain, like Tommy's Felicity — English, upper class, an artist — in Spain fighting for the workers, but none surprised us more than Jewish Cockney Sammy Cohen. A Jew in Spain — in Spain for Christ's sake — not a country exactly full of happy memories for the Jewish people after all — but there he was. A volunteer. A member of the International Brigade. How could I be anywhere else but where I am now, having met the likes of Sammy? It would be an insult to his memory if I wasn't here continuing the fight he fought and died for. God, when I think of the darkness I went through after Spain. That's not to say it can't be dark here sometimes — especially without you, for, though I know you hate me to say it, it was you who helped me through that darkness. It was you who helped me shake off the despair I found in myself. It was you who helped me to love again. Despair is a selfish state and if praying was my way I'd pray that such a state of self-obsession will never return again. Loving you will keep it at bay, Miriam. Give kisses and hugs to wee Rachel and my Ma and to you, my love, everything. Love, Billy.

Light off Billy.
Miriam sits. A tear rolls down her cheek.
Silence.
Enter Rachel and Rosie.

RACHEL: Mummy! Mummy! Look what Rosie bought me.

Rachel displays whip and pirry. Miriam gathers herself and hurriedly puts letter in pocket.

MIRIAM: Oh my! And can you do it? Show Mummy.

Rachel tries without much success.

ROSIE: Practice will make perfect, Rachel, don't you worry. It takes a while to get the hang of it. God, I remember the first one of those my mother, God rest her, bought for me. I was maybe only half your size, Rachel.

RACHEL: Why were you crying, Mummy?

MIRIAM: Was I?

RACHEL: Did you get a letter from Daddy? When is he coming to live with us and Rosie?

Miriam and Rosie exchange looks.

ROSIE: Rachel love, didn't that wee girl down the street . . . what's her name now?

RACHEL: Mary.

ROSIE: Mary, that's it. Didn't she say she wanted to play with you before it got dark? Why don't you go and show her your new perry and whip?

RACHEL: Can I, Mummy?

MIRIAM: Of course, Rachel. But don't stay away too long. Rosie and I get lonely without you.

Rachel goes to door to exit.

RACHEL: Sometimes, Mummy, I get lonely without Daddy.

Rachel turns and exits.
Miriam looks to Rosie.

ROSIE: You know, Miriam, that wee girl of ours has an older head on her than her seven years.

MIRIAM: How did she. . .

ROSIE: Never underestimate children or the clergy, my mother used to say. They know more than we give them credit for most times. The clergy mightn't marry but they're hard to shock in the confessional. And children? Well, children have a nose for things all their own.

MIRIAM: Your mother was right, I think, Rosie.

Miriam fingering letter in her pocket.

ROSIE: You were crying, love, weren't you? Want to talk about it?

MIRIAM: I had a letter from Billy.

ROSIE: I know. So had I. They both arrived together this morning. Our Billy's handwriting on both envelopes. He seems in right form. I haven't heard him so jaunty since he wrote me when he first went to Spain. Though, God love him, I'm sure there's not much to be jaunty about fighting Nazis.

MIRIAM: No. . .

Rosie sits down facing Miriam.
Pause.

ROSIE: You're in love with our Billy, aren't you, Miriam?

Miriam looks hesitant.

ROSIE: I *know* you are, Miriam. It's not a thing women can hide. Men try but they're see-through as the rest of us. I knew it would happen. I could see it in our Billy's eyes the first day he met you.

MIRIAM: You could?

ROSIE: I'm his mother, Miriam. I brought him into the world. I wiped his arse for him the first years of his life. There's not much you can hide from somebody who does that for you. Men forget that. They think they were always big, independent men. Huh! They make me laugh sometimes with the stances they take up. Look at Jimmy. Jimmy's still like a wee lad who's had his bag of sweets confiscated. A hero of 1916. The war against the Tans. The Civil War. And he behaves like he's hardly out of nappies.

Miriam smiles. Pause.

MIRIAM: But how did you know about me. . .?

ROSIE: You? Oh, you were a dead giveaway as well. I knew you were falling in love with Billy the night you asked could you go walking with him after that ding-dong session with Jimmy about Ireland and neutrality. Ach, God, Miriam, you're not surprised I know?

MIRIAM: No, Rosie. No. . .

ROSIE: It's hardly a surprise in times like these we're living in. And you're not unusual. I'm sure it's happening all over Europe. People thrown together in the most bizarre circumstances. I sometimes think it's only in the event of a war or a similar catastrophe that we fall in love with who we really want to fall in love with. Passion flourishes in time of danger, Miriam.

MIRIAM: Did it with you, Rosie?

ROSIE: Christ, it must have been something like that for how else could I put up with the likes of Jimmy now if I didn't have the memory of the first flood? I joke now, Miriam, about it, but then I was *mad* for him. Hungry for him. It was a craving I had no control over. The Civil War was on. I never knew if I would ever see him again from one grabbed moment of leave to the next. And God, was it exciting, Miriam. Death and Sex. The contrary couple. But Christ, I wouldn't have missed out on it for all the tea in China.

MIRIAM: And now?

ROSIE: Now? Like I told you, I'm living with a shattered man with a shattered dream. But I love him for having had that dream. I love him for what was, what we had, and what we gave to each other. For while Jimmy and I are still alive and together, the past is not dead. The dream is not dead. Besides, before you arrived I was living with two shattered men, but things have improved by half.

MIRIAM: You don't disapprove then?

ROSIE: Of what?

MIRIAM: Of Billy and me?

ROSIE: Disapprove of love? How could I, knowing what it is?

MIRIAM: I *do* love him, Rosie.

ROSIE: I hope you *do*. And I hope *he* loves you.

MIRIAM: He does. He does.

Silence.

MIRIAM: Love . . . doesn't stop me having a husband, Rosie. I still do have a husband and you heard Rachel asking for her daddy.

ROSIE: Do you love *him*, Miriam? Do you love your husband?

MIRIAM: I think . . . I did . . . once. But it's been so long, and I have no idea where he is. I don't know if he's alive or. . .

ROSIE: Dead?

MIRIAM: If only I knew one way or the other. . .

ROSIE: And if you did, Miriam, would it stop you loving Billy?

MIRIAM: No. Never. Nothing could ever stop me loving Billy.

> *Enter Billy in uniform. Stands in doorway arms out-stretched. Smiling. Miriam runs towards him. Blackout.*

3 SCENE

N.B. This is a split scene.
We see 'events' in Robinson kitchen and Billy and Miriam in exterior scene simultaneously. Black Mountain. Billy and Miriam looking out over city.

MIRIAM: It's beautiful up here, Billy. What is it you call it again?

BILLY: The Black Mountain.

MIRIAM: The Black Mountain! Look, you can see the whole of Belfast city below us.

BILLY: Belfast. Do you see the shipyard with the cranes away on the left there? You know, there's not many Taigs work in yon!

MIRIAM: (*Laughs*) Not many Jews either I imagine.

BILLY: No. But it was founded by a Jew. Well, half-founded — the Woolf of Harland and Woolf is Jewish. Came here to Belfast in 1858, I think.

MIRIAM: (*In mock Belfast*) Do you think maybe I could get a start if I told him I was a cousin?

> *Billy laughs and puts his arm round Miriam. They look out.*

Cut to Robinson kitchen. Rachel is sitting beside Rosie who is reading to her.
Pause. Enter two men.

FIRST MAN: The door was open, Mrs Robinson.

ROSIE: It always is. Who are you? What do you want?

SECOND MAN: We're friends of Jimmy's, Mrs Robinson.

ROSIE: Oh aye? Well, he's not in. You'll probably find him ensconced in the bar of McGlinchey's.

FIRST MAN: Aye. We know that, Mrs Robinson.

SECOND MAN: We just left him there you see.

ROSIE: So what are you looking for him here for then?

Cut to Black Mountain.

MIRIAM: I like Belfast, Billy. I like the people.

BILLY: You do? Aye, I suppose there's worse. It's not a bad aul' city. At any rate, it's mine for better or worse.

MIRIAM: It's mine too now, Billy. And Rachel's. She's having a great time, you know.

BILLY: She's still hitting it off with my Ma then?

MIRIAM: Like tweedledum and tweedledee they are. Your mother is very good to her. She's very good to both of us. She's a very remarkable woman your mother, Billy.

BILLY: My Ma? Yeh, she's the heart of corn. She's a bloody saint putting up with my Da all these years.

MIRIAM: She loves him.

Miriam smiles at Billy. They kiss.
Cut to:

FIRST MAN: Is Billy in?

SECOND MAN: Billy. Your son, Mrs Robinson.

ROSIE: I know who my own son is. What do you want with him?

FIRST MAN: Just a bit of a yarn.

SECOND MAN: A wee chat. That's all, Mrs Robinson.

ROSIE: Are you friends of Billy's as well?

Two men exchange looks.

FIRST MAN: In a manner of speaking . . . yes.

SECOND MAN: Yes. You could say that. You could say we're 'friends' of Billy's.

ROSIE: Well, he's not in either.

FIRST MAN: Where is he, Mrs Robinson?

ROSIE: Well, if he's not in, I suppose he must be out!

FIRST MAN: Whereabouts? Out?

Cut to:

BILLY: And how has Jimmy been? Behaving himself is he, my Da?

MIRIAM: We hardly see him. He's either at work or in. . .

BILLY: McGlinchey's bar.

MIRIAM: Yes.

BILLY: It's a wonder he hasn't the place bought out after all this time. Or drunk it dry. But he's not giving you any aul' lip these days?

MIRIAM: No. He's not. I tell you, Billy, we hardly ever see him.

BILLY: Does he ever mention me? Is there ever any word of his 'soldier' son?

MIRIAM: Not to me there isn't. Well he wouldn't, would he? I don't know what he says to your mother, but she has passed no remark on it.

Cut to:

ROSIE: Look! What is this all about? I've never seen you men before. Are you sure you're friends of Jimmy's? Who are you? What's your names?

FIRST MAN: Oh, we're friends of Jimmy's alright.

SECOND MAN: You see, you could say, Jimmy sent us in a way.

ROSIE: He did?

FIRST MAN: To look for Billy.

SECOND MAN: To have a yarn with him.

FIRST MAN: But you say Billy's *out*.

ROSIE: I told you so. I don't boil my cabbage twice.

SECOND MAN: And who'd he be *out* with, Mrs Robinson?

Cut to:

MIRIAM: I feel so happy, Billy. I don't know when I last felt such happiness. To be here, with you.

BILLY: You're very beautiful, Miriam. I love you.

MIRIAM: I love you, Billy. How I love you.

They kiss passionately and fall to ground, laugh and then in silence stare at each other.
Cut to:

FIRST MAN: Who's he with, Mrs Robinson?

ROSIE: What business is that of yours?

FIRST MAN: Plenty, Mrs Robinson. Plenty!

SECOND MAN: Is he out with that Englishwoman you have staying here?

ROSIE: I think it's time you two gentlemen left, if you don't mind.

RACHEL: Rosie! Read to me again. I want you to read to me.

ROSIE: Yes, Rachel. In a minute, love. These gentlemen are just leaving, *now*.

FIRST MAN: Hello Rachel.

Rachel stares at two men.

SECOND MAN: Pretty child, Mrs Robinson. She wouldn't be the daughter of that Jewish slut you have boarding here?

ROSIE: Get out! Get the hell out of here before I take the poker to the both of ye. . .

Rosie lifts poker. First man grabs her arm, takes poker from her and pushes her back into sofa.

RACHEL: Rosie! Tell the men to go away. I don't like them, Rosie.

ROSIE: It's alright Rachel. They're leaving now.

First man fingers British Army uniform hanging from wall.
Silence.
Cut to:

MIRIAM: Make love to me, Billy. I want you.

BILLY: What? Here? Now? Half way up the Black Mountain?

MIRIAM: Yes. Now. Half way up the Black Mountain. Make love to me, Billy . . . with the city of Belfast below us . . . your city . . . my city. . . Our city. . .

Cut to:
Events in Robinson home, but in silhouette we are aware of
Billy and Miriam disrobing.

FIRST MAN: So this is what a brand new British Army uniform looks like. Not bad cloth. You know, I've never seen one so close before.

SECOND MAN: Does your son Billy look good in it, Mrs Robinson? Nothing like a man in uniform, eh?

FIRST MAN: An *Irishman* in a British uniform!

Second man takes down uniform from wall.

ROSIE: Put that down, you wee skitter. . .

First man forces Rosie back onto sofa.

SECOND MAN: Defending the King and Empire, Mrs Robinson?

FIRST MAN: Just like your son, Billy. . .

ROSIE: Get out. Get out. You no good pair of scallywags. If Jimmy knew. . .

SECOND MAN: Oh, but he knows alright, Mrs Robinson. *He knows.*

FIRST MAN: He sent us, Mrs Robinson.

SECOND MAN: Poor Jimmy! Imagine having a wife who harbours an Englishwoman. And a son who betrays his own country and fucks with a yid. A married yid at that. . .

Sound of Billy and Miriam.

FIRST MAN: Where's your Jewish daddy then, Rachel?

Rachel begins to cry.

ROSIE: *You animal!*

SECOND MAN: Maybe she hasn't got a daddy. Have you got a daddy, Rachel?

FIRST MAN: Is your mammy out fucking with an Irish traitor?

Sound of Billy and Miriam making love. Rosie goes for first man. Second man grabs her from behind. First man seems about to hit her with poker, but doesn't. Second man still holds her from behind. Rachel runs out door.

ROSIE: Rachel . . . Rachel. . .

Second man still holds on to Rosie. While first man rips

*apart army uniform and throws it onto floor in pieces and
spits on it. Second man throws Rosie aside.*
Pause.
They make to leave.

FIRST MAN: Don't forget to tell Billy we called, Mrs Robinson.

Exit two men.
*Final image — Rosie sitting on chair, shocked. Silhouette
of two lovers lying side by side.*
Blackout.

SCENE 4

*Robinson home. Same as at end of Scene 3. Billy's ripped uniform
lying on floor.*
Silence.
Enter Miriam. She looks around room — worried.

MIRIAM: Billy!

Enter Billy.

BILLY: What the hell has been going on here. . .?

He picks up bits of uniform.

MIRIAM: Who could have done such a thing, Billy? Who was
here?

BILLY: Ma! Ma!

*Billy goes into scullery, out back into yard, calling his
mother.*

MIRIAM: Rachel! Rosie!

Billy returns to kitchen.

BILLY: Stay here, Miriam. I'll check upstairs.

Billy exits. Miriam, holding piece of uniform, slumps into chair. Her expression tells us something about whole history of such events.
Billy returns. Miriam looks at him questioningly. Worried. Anxious.

BILLY: Nothing. Everything as normal.

Pause.

MIRIAM: Who, Billy? Who?

Enter Rosie excited and flustered.

ROSIE: You're back. Thank God for that.

MIRIAM: Where's Rachel?

Small pause.

ROSIE: I don't know, Miriam. I don't know. I've been looking for her everywhere. Searched all the places she might be. Called at Mrs Maguires' and Mrs Boyle's. But we'll find her, Miriam. We'll find her, love.

Rosie puts arm round Miriam who sits, stunned.

BILLY: What happened, Ma? Who was here?

ROSIE: I don't know.

BILLY: What do you mean you don't know?

ROSIE: I mean I don't know their names, Billy. Two men — about your age. They said they were looking for you.

BILLY: Were they now?

ROSIE: They started making cracks about traitors. They were talking about you, Billy, and about me. Harbouring an 'Englishwoman' they said. They called Miriam. . .

MIRIAM: Go on, Rosie. . .

BILLY: What did they say Ma?

ROSIE: They called her a Jewish slut. . .

Billy paces angrily with fists clenched.

ROSIE: Then they started going on to the child. . .

MIRIAM: Rachel?

ROSIE: They asked her where her daddy was and did she have a daddy and was her mammy out . . . 'fucking' with an Irish traitor? That's what they said to the child. O Mother of God . . . to the child. . .

BILLY: Did they take Rachel, Ma?

ROSIE: No. No. I went for one of them with the poker . . . Rachel ran out . . . they pushed me about . . . then they saw your uniform and ripped it apart . . . then as cool as you like just as they walked in, they walked out, saying . . . tell Billy we called. Tell, Billy. . . As soon as they'd gone, I ran out, looking, searching for Rachel. But I couldn't find her . . . I couldn't find her. I'm sorry, Miriam . . . I'm sorry. . .

Rosie breaks down in tears.

BILLY: It's alright, Ma. We'll find her. We'll find Rachel.

ROSIE: But that's not all, Billy. That's not all. The dream . . . the dream . . . the dream is shattered . . . it's dead. Dead and buried.

BILLY: What are you talking about, Ma? What dream?

ROSIE: Billy . . . they said your father sent them. They said they were 'friends' of Jimmy's. The dream . . . dead . . . dead and buried. . .

BILLY: Ma? Where is my Da?

ROSIE: I don't know. I don't know, Billy. But they said they were talking to him. . .

BILLY: In McGlinchey's?

Rosie nods.

ROSIE: Oh, Miriam. Miriam, love. What have I brought you into?

Billy puts on jacket.

MIRIAM: Billy? Billy? Where are you going? What are you going to do?

ROSIE: No, Billy. No. They're not worth it. We must find Rachel. That's the most important thing. Rachel. We must find the child.

Enter Rachel.

RACHEL: Mummy! Mummy!

Rachel runs to her mother.

MIRIAM: *Rachel!*

ROSIE: God and His Holy Mother be praised. You answered my prayers, St Anthony. Bless you.

RACHEL: The men came, Mummy. I was frightened. They hit Rosie. I ran away. I was hiding.

MIRIAM: It's alright, now, Rachel. Mummy's here. And Rosie. And Billy.

Miriam takes Rachel over to Rosie. They cluster in an embrace.

RACHEL: Did the bad men hurt you, Rosie?

ROSIE: No, love. No. Rosie's well now. Now that Rachel's here.

BILLY: I'll be back shortly. Stay here. And whatever you do, don't move out of the house. Lock the door after me.

Miriam gets up.

MIRIAM: Billy?

Billy kisses her.

BILLY: I won't be long. I love you.

Exit Billy.
Miriam turns, she and Rosie exchange looks.
Slow fade.

5   SCENE

McGlinchey's bar. Jimmy and Billy.

BILLY: Hello, Da. What are you having? The usual?

Jimmy looks at Billy slightly surprised.

JIMMY: I have one in front of me, can't you see?

BILLY: Never known you to refuse another, Da. A half 'un?

JIMMY: No. Thanks.

BILLY: Are you sure?

JIMMY: I *said*. . .

BILLY: Alright, alright. Whatever you say yourself.
Drinks business.
Pause.

JIMMY: I'm surprised at you showing your face in here, Billy.

BILLY: Really? Why's that, Da?

JIMMY: They're not fond of serving the King's Men in here, that's why!

BILLY: Well, they serve you, Da, don't they? And have been doing for years now.

JIMMY: What's that supposed to mean? I'm not a British soldier. Or haven't you noticed?

BILLY: Oh aye. I've noticed alright. I've noticed.
Pause.

BILLY: But what are you, Da? What exactly are you?

JIMMY: It's time you finished that pint and were on your way, lad.

BILLY: You haven't answered my question, 'Father'.

JIMMY: And I'm not going to, 'Son'.

BILLY: Why's that? Why's that? Would the answer be too painful?

JIMMY: I told you to be on your way.

BILLY: What is it, Da? Would it take *guts* to hear the answer to what you are? Would it take you to have a strong stomach, Mr Robinson?

JIMMY: Not something you're known for, Billy, now is it? A strong stomach?

BILLY: So you've told me, Father. So you've told me. But methinks it must run in the family . . . if it's true, you understand.

JIMMY: Now, listen here, Billy, don't you come in here with any of your aul' lip or insinuations. If you were half the man I am. . .

BILLY: That would be no man at all, wouldn't it, Da? For I don't think you're a man at all. In fact, I'm not sure what sort of a specimen you are . . . but whatever it is it's pretty bloody low in the evolutionary scale of things.

JIMMY: Get out! Get the fuck out of here. Now!

BILLY: When I'm ready, specimen. When I'm ready. I haven't finished telling you what sort of specimen I think you really are.

Jimmy turns to grab Billy, but Billy grips Jimmy's arm tight. Hold on. Grimly.

BILLY: You're a cowardly specimen, Da. A yellow belly. A skunk. All those things you said I was. You're the lowest of the low . . . for any *man* who would send round two of his 'patriot' friends to intimidate and knock about his own wife is a gutless spineless first class bastard. . .

JIMMY: And is that what you're having with that Yiddish hussy who's been fouling my home the stench is so bad I can't spend time in my own house? Another little Jew bastard to play with the one she's already got. . .

Drinks spill. Glasses break.
Enter the two men.

FIRST MAN: Everything alright, Mister Robinson?

BILLY: Ho Ho. Look what the wind's blew in. Aren't you going to introduce me to your two 'patriot' friends, Da?

Jimmy nods to men not to take action.

BILLY: I understand you two gentlemen were looking for me earlier on. Well, here I am. What's the message?

SECOND MAN: I think maybe it's time you left, Billy Robinson.

BILLY: Yeh. I think you are probably right. The smell in here has become distinctly green and bile-like. It has that shitty patriotic bouquet about it.

First man takes step towards Billy. Jimmy steps between them.

BILLY: You amaze me, Da. Don't tell me you're going to soil your pure Irish hands with your own dirty work.

JIMMY: On your way, Billy. Before. . .

BILLY: Before what, Da? Before what? Before you set the

saviours of Ireland onto your own son. . .? Your own flesh and blood. . .?

JIMMY: There's nothing of mine in you, Billy.

BILLY: You said it. The final statement. I'm going. And gladly. For there's nothing you have I'd want. Not you. Not them. Not any of what's here. You can keep your little Western isle. You can keep your dark bog-drenched vision. You can have it. I give it to you all on a platter. If this is Ireland I want no part of it. Fuck you! And fuck Ireland!

Two men make for Billy. In skirmish, Billy manages to hit first man while second man inadvertently chins Jimmy. Jimmy lying on floor, hand to mouth, looks up at Billy.

BILLY: Goodbye, Da!

Blackout.

SCENE 6

Belfast docks. Rosie, Miriam, Rachel and Billy with suitcases.

RACHEL: Is this the place, Rosie, where Mummy and me got off the boat?

ROSIE: Yes, Rachel, love. It is. And little did I think then I would be getting on the boat with you and your Mummy.

RACHEL: I'm glad you're coming on the big boat, Rosie.

ROSIE: And leaving. Leaving Belfast . . . leaving Ireland.

BILLY: You'll be back, Ma.

ROSIE: Will I? Will I, Billy?

MIRIAM: Of course you will, Rosie. After all this is over, you'll be . . . we'll be back. . .

ROSIE: I don't think so, Miriam. I don't think I'll ever be back again. (*Pause*) What would I come back to? (*To Billy*) Your father? (*To Miriam*) Back to Jimmy?

Pause.

RACHEL: Mummy, will Daddy be waiting for us in England?

Lights come up, silhouetting Jimmy sitting in armchair by fireside.

RACHEL: Will he, Mummy? Will he?

Billy and Miriam exchange look.

BILLY: C'mon, Rachel. Take Rosie's hand. It's time we were all on that big boat. Will you look after Rosie for Billy, Rachel? She's never been on a big boat before, you know.

Rachel takes Rosie's hand. Billy and Miriam lift suitcases. Anxious. Worried.

RACHEL: Rosie?

Pause.

ROSIE: Yes, Rachel?

RACHEL: What's a war?

All freeze. Hold in half light.
Lights on Jimmy.
Pause.
Sound of German planes overhead, over Belfast.
Jimmy looks up.
Hold. Slow fade.

THE MURPHY GIRLS

**A play
in 15 scenes**

THE MURPHY GIRLS was first performed in June 1988 at the Drill Hall Arts Centre, London.

CAST

BRID MURPHY	Gerardine Hinds
NORA MURPHY	Mary Duddy
AINE MURPHY	Kate O'Connell
TOMMY MURPHY	James Greene
CAITLIN MURPHY	Jenny Bolt
PATRICK O'BRIEN	Allan Radcliffe

Other parts played by the cast.
The play was directed by Julia Pascal.

CHARACTERS

BRID MURPHY
R.U.C. SPECIAL BRANCH OFFICER
NORA MURPHY
AINE MURPHY
TOMMY MURPHY
CAITLIN MURPHY
PAT O'BRIEN
R.U.C. POLICEWOMAN
R.U.C. INSPECTOR
AN ENGLISHMAN
ENGLISH SPECIAL BRANCH OFFICER
A SOLDIER

PROLOGUE

House lights down.

TAPE/VOICE: Ladies and Gentlemen, we are about to land at Aldergrove Airport, Belfast. Kindly extinguish your cigarettes and refrain from smoking until you are inside the terminal building. You are advised to remain seated with your seat belts fastened until after the aircraft has come to a complete standstill. Thank you for flying British Airways Supershuttle this morning. We hope you enjoyed your flight and we look forward to seeing you again soon. Thank you and goodbye.

SCENE 1

Aldergrove Airport, Northern Ireland. Brid Murphy and R.U.C. Special Branch Officer. Brid is carrying a suitcase or travel bag.

OFFICER: Identification, Miss?

Brid opens handbag, takes out Irish passport. Hands it to officer.

OFFICER: What's your address, Miss Murphy?

BRID: Isn't it written on that?

OFFICER: Can you *tell* me your address please, Miss Murphy?

BRID: 14 Kentish Town Avenue, London NW5.

OFFICER: And your date of birth?

BRID: 15th November, 1949.

OFFICER: What's the purpose of your visit to Northern Ireland, Miss Murphy?

BRID: To visit my parents.

OFFICER: A holiday, eh?

BRID: Makes a change from the Mediterranean, don't you think?

OFFICER: Your parents' address?

BRID: 9 Milltown Park, West Belfast.

OFFICER: And how long do you intend staying in Northern Ireland?

BRID: I haven't decided. Few days. Maybe a week. Maybe. . .

Officer returns passport to Brid.

OFFICER: I hope you enjoy your holiday in West Belfast, Brid!

Hold. Blackout.
Sound/Music.

2 SCENE

The Murphy home. Brid with travel bag.

BRID: Hello! Anybody home? It's me. I'm here. Hello.

Silence.

Nothing like a welcoming party is there?

Brid removes coat. Looks around room. Picks up photo. Replaces. Sits down at table. Begins flicking through Andersonstown News. Republican News newspapers lying on table.

Silence.

Enter Mrs Nora Murphy.

NORA: Jesus Mary and Joseph, you nearly scared the wits out of me there, Brid love. How are you doing? I didn't expect you so soon.

Mother and daughter embrace.

BRID: Hello, Mother. Good to see you. You're looking well.

NORA: Do you think so? What do you think of my hair? It's not too much with the streaks, is it?

BRID: Not at all. It's very nice.

NORA: Sure, that's what kept me. You know I always go up to the hairdressers on a Friday morning. Well, I go to ten Mass first and then Gina, that's the hairdresser, keeps an appointment for me for about eleven. Sure, I thought I'd be down home before you arrived. Was your plane early or what?

BRID: No. It was more or less on time. But I was delayed a bit coming out off the airport by this ever so charming Special Branch Officer.

NORA: I hope you didn't cheek him or anything, Brid. They don't need encouragement these days to turn nasty.

BRID: Now, Mother, really! Would I give lip to the forces of law and order?

NORA: You must've changed if you didn't for you used to give plenty to me, I know that.

BRID: Telling me off for the past and me just arrived home, Mother?

Mother and daughter banteringly embrace.

NORA: Away on with you, our Brid. Sit down there and I'll make us a wee cup of tea. Did you take the bus in from the airport?

BRID: No. I took a taxi. There was no Ulsterbuses to be seen.

NORA: Everybody coming in from that airport says the same. But those buses are supposed to be there to meet the flights coming in. What did the taxi man charge you?

BRID: Nine pound. I gave him a tenner.

NORA: Oh, aye, you would. And them has a lot more money than you'll ever have.

BRID: I think he was a Protestant.

NORA: How do you know?

BRID: He turned a whiter shade of pale when I gave him the address of where I wanted to go. 'And where exactly is that, Miss?', says he. 'Oh just head for Andytown and I'll direct you from there', says I. Poor cratur nearly choked, but he didn't say no.

NORA: Don't kid yourself, those fellas would drive to hell if they thought there was a fare in it.

BRID: He became quite chatty once he discovered I lived in London. Out of it, you see. No threat. Not a local native anymore. Told me all about his daughter being a nurse and working in London for a while before she married a Scotsman. Lives in Aberdeen now. Two children. I didn't ask if the hubbie was a squaddie. I rose in his estimation when I told him I was a teacher. You could see his eyes say 'she's an educated Catholic, and had the good sense to get out. Nice wee girl. Very well spoken for a Taig!' He'd been in London. Didn't like it. 'An awful rat race,' says he. 'No. When you come to my time in life' (he was about sixty) 'the pace of life in Ireland is what suits. And to tell you the truth, Miss, I'm not overfond of the English people', says he. He gave me a sideways glance at that point, and we smiled knowingly at each other. Brid Murphy and the Proddie taxi man. Comrades for life!

NORA: No wonder you gave him the quid tip, 'Comrade'. Oh, he saw you coming alright, Brid Murphy. Here y'ar. Here's the tea. I'm sure you're hungry, are you not? Have one of those baps. I just got them fresh from McErleans on the way down home.

Tea business.

BRID: How's my father? And Aine and Caitlin?

NORA: Aine's fine. Still teaching away at St Dominic's. Mind you, I think she does too much for them. All those extra-curricular activities she does with the sixth form and that. And I've always said — 'the nuns'll exploit you if they see you're willing'. But you know Aine, she says she doesn't do it for the nuns but for the girls themselves. But I'd like to see her take it easy a bit more. You can be over-dedicated, I think. And there's no sign of a man in her life — least none I know about, and you'd soon hear in this place if she was stepping out with somebody. My mother used to say you couldn't break wind on the Falls Road but the Bishop would know about it before nightfall.

BRID: And Caitlin?

NORA: She's expectin' again.

BRID: She's what?

NORA: God, did I not mention it to you on the phone?

BRID: No. You did not, Mother.

NORA: Well, she's only just had it confirmed. I musta forgot to tell you, what with all the excitement and talk about you coming home. It's over a year since you were here, you know, Brid Murphy.

BRID: What's she hoping for this time?

NORA: I think she'd like a wee girl having had the two boys. But his mother had all boys, you know, so the odds are. . .

BRID: It'll be another boy! Is she keeping well?

NORA: You know our Caitlin. Is there anything ever knocks her out of gear? She seems to take everything in her stride. Mind you, she has a good man to support her. Sometimes I think she takes Sean too much for granted. Many's another man. . .

BRID: Don't talk nonsense, Mother. Why should it be a surprise when a man behaves as he should?

NORA: Because, Brid, too often they don't. There's a brave few of them round here and it would shock you the goings-on of them — married or not!

BRID: Talking of men, how's my father? Is he indulging in goings-on?

NORA: Your father? When would he have the time? Politics is your father's mistress and in many ways a far more dangerous and boring creature than any 'other woman'. To tell you the truth, he has my head turned. For there's not a mealtime passes when he doesn't rant and roar about 'the situation'. The Anglo-Irish Agreement, Haughey, Maggie, the Provies, the Birmingham Six, Stalker, Gibraltar, the nurses, the miners, the Palestinians. . .

BRID: But what's wrong with talking about those things, Mother?

NORA: Nothing, Brid. If talking was what he did. But he doesn't *talk* — he rants and roars and works himself up into a red-faced frenzy. I sometimes think he'll take a coronary in front of me. And then what happens? What will politics do for him then? Neither your father nor I is getting any younger, Brid, and I would like to spend what years is spared to us living with a bit of peace and quiet — with the time to enjoy and take pleasure in my grandchildren — not always going from heated debate to heated argument all the bloody time over events that neither I nor your father has any control over. We'll be pushing up the daisies for a long time after and the world will continue to be full of politics and politicians. But never mind all that now. What about you? What's your news? No word of you getting married yet?

BRID: Mother?

NORA: It would please your father you know if you did. . .

BRID: But Mother, I stopped doing things to *please* people a long time ago. If I'd wanted to *please* people, I would never have left Ireland and gone to live in London.

NORA: You know, Brid, Irish men like your father, for all their shouting and screaming on political matters, can be deeply conservative about other things.

BRID: Other things?

NORA: You know. Men. Women. Sex. They don't really realize that people of your generation have shunned their way of doing things. They certainly don't think it happens in their own families. Yes, they read about it in the newspapers,

but they certainly don't consider it happens with girls —
daughters — if you were a boy, Brid, your father would
understand better. . .

BRID: Would he? Then he's an even bigger hypocrite than I
thought.

NORA: But can't you see how hard it is for him, Brid? That his
daughter, reared at convents, leaves home and goes to
London and then lives with a man outside of marriage. It's
hard for me, Brid. It goes against my Catholic religion.
But I'm a woman and women, I think, are better at
adapting to reality than men. I don't like what you've
done but I can accept it. But your father. . .

BRID: But Mother, it's not a question of him or you accepting it,
understanding it, or anything else. What I do is what *I* do.
It's my business, decided upon by me. I'm not interested
in being understood or accepted, I just want to be left
alone to get on with my life my way. I don't want to be told
how I should live my life by anyone — you, my father, the
Holy Roman Empire or the Pope himself. I left Ireland
because. . .

NORA: God, Brid, you talk quare and funny sometimes for
someone who was educated by the Dominican nuns.

BRID: Maybe it's because of my Dominican education that I talk
the way I do.

NORA: Do you never go to Mass now at all?

BRID: No, Mother. Never.

NORA: So, it's true what the clergy say — when the young people
go to England, they lose their faith.

BRID: Mother, I had lost 'my faith' long before I went to
England. And the Irish clergy maybe should examine
their Irish Christianity for the fault rather than blaming
England for all Ireland's ills.

NORA: She's to blame for most of them. . .

BRID: Is she, Mother? Is she? Not from where I stand.

NORA: In England, you mean!

BRID: Maybe you need to get out to have clear vision. But you
know, Mother, for this place to be so full of Catholics,

there's damn little evidence of too many examining their consciences about anything.

NORA: And who are you, Brid Murphy, to say that? Maybe they are, in their own way, and maybe like you they don't want to be told by anyone else how to do it.

Enter Aine.

AINE: Politics and religion, is it? That's one thing about this house, you don't have to be in it long until you're stuck in up to your oxters in arguing and debating.

BRID: Aine! How are you? Good to see you, big sister.

Embrace.

AINE: Hello, Brid. I'm glad to see you looking so well and in your usual cornaptious form. Mother, I've told you before not to pay any attention to what the likes of this one says and does, for though she'll hate me to say it, but she's like her father. She's a chip off my Da alright. She lives and breathes conflict. They're both of a kind, Mother. It's only you and me are the balanced human beings around here.

NORA: I think maybe you're right, Aine. I just know I've had enough of all this conflict. Twenty bloody years of it! How was school the day, love?

AINE: Great. Fridays always are. You go round high in the knowledge that there are two days without school about to happen.

NORA: Would you like a cup of tea?

BRID: I'll make it. You sit there. How about a cup of coffee?

AINE: Real coffee?

BRID: Of course. I brought some with me.

NORA: Not for me, thanks. I wouldn't thank you for coffee. Tea'll do me fine. You never used to drink coffee before you went to England. And if you did, Nescafé would've done you. But oh no, not now. It has to be real coffee. Christ, it's amazing your father and I managed to rear three daughters at all and without going anywhere and without a college education. (*Angry and tearful*) I think I'll go up and lie down for a while before your father arrives in for his dinner. No doubt there'll be another session of parliament amongst yiz then, too. I'm sick of it. Sick of it!

BRID: Will I bring you up a cup of tea?

NORA: Whatever you like. Do as you do.

Exit Nora.
Pause.

AINE: What was all that about? How long have yiz been at it then?

Brid shrugs.

BRID: It started with 'Is there no word of you getting married yet?'

AINE: Is that all? I wish I had a fiver for every time that question was pointed at me. I'd be able to retire immediately with a fortune.

BRID: And what's the answer, sister? Is there any word of you getting married?

AINE: Away on with ye, Brid Murphy. I'll not ask you if you don't ask me.

BRID: Well, is there anybody on the go?

AINE: Brid! (*Pause*) How's your English lover?

BRID: Fuck off, Aine.

They laugh together.

AINE: Whatever he's doing to you it suits you. You're looking great.

BRID: Thanks. You're not looking bad yourself. Remarkably well, in fact, given you spend most of your life within the confines of that bloody convent school that I couldn't wait to escape from.

AINE: Old Mother Peter was asking for you. I told her you were coming home for a holiday.

BRID: Christ, is that aul witch still alive?

AINE: I like witches myself, sister. And she was very complimentary in her memories of you. 'One of the very best history students I ever had was Brid Murphy. Of course I didn't teach you, Aine. You were a literature student, were you not? Of course you were. You're Head of the English Department now aren't you?'

BRID: Mother Peter. She knew her subject, I'll give her that. But what an aul snob she was. Her people were loaded with money, you know. They owned property all over the place. No doubt they used to collect rents on half the slum houses on the Falls Road. And then she acted the Dominican Our Lady over the offspring of those her family fed on. God, it's a wonderfully Christian country Ireland but then its sickness is 'all England's fault'!

AINE: Pardon?

BRID: Oh, nothing. Just something Mother and I were chewing at.

AINE: So how long are you home for this time?

BRID: A week maybe.

AINE: And how come your school is closed?

BRID: Jewish holidays.

AINE: And how is it with them these days? Must be fairly lively, what with the Middle East situation and that.

BRID: It's stimulating.

AINE: I'd avoid mentioning it in front of my Da if I were you. His state of mind these days has the British Army, the Israelis and Sir John Hermon all wrapped up in the one parcel.

BRID: Yeh. And I suspect he's not the only one in the 32 Counties to be pronouncing self-righteously on something he knows nothing about. I read in the *Irish Times* about the Friends of Palestine in Dublin protesting about the Zionist State. Strange that, and they can hardly open their mouths about what's happening in their own backyard.

AINE: Well, Brid, you know what Joyce said. That it was only because there were no Jews in Ireland that the Irish were not anti-Semitic.

BRID: And the few Jews that were here were attacked and hounded from Limerick in 1904, at the behest of — surprise surprise — a Redemptorist priest.

AINE: I didn't know that, Brid.

BRID: You learn a lot teaching in a Jewish school. I bet my Da doesn't know it either. And I bet he doesn't know that those fighting to found Israel were influenced by Irish Republicans.

AINE: You're kidding me?

BRID: No kidding. Little Itzak Shamir is a fan of the big fellow — Michael Collins. Seems the likes of Shamir and Begin studied our fellows' techniques for bumping off British Intelligence Officers. But then that's not something you'd read in the *Republican News* now, is it? Mind you, it's not something you'd read in the *Jewish Chronicle* either.

Enter Tommy Murphy.

TOMMY: What isn't? What wouldn't I read in the *Republican News*? And sure if I couldn't read it there, can it be worth reading, I ask myself? Hello, Aine, love. And Brid. Well, how's the Murphy in exile getting on? You're looking well. They must have changed the air over in England for you to have such a bloom on your cheeks.

BRID: Hello, Daddy.

TOMMY: And doesn't the old man of Ireland get a kiss from his distant daughter?

They embrace.

TOMMY: Powerful well you're looking, Brid, daughter. Isn't she, Aine?

AINE: Blooming as you say, Father.

TOMMY: God, your mother and I reared powerful good-looking women. And there they are, keeping their beauty to themselves. Too precious is it to share with a man?

Hold/fade.

SCENE 2A

Tommy, Nora, Aine, Brid. They have just finished dinner. Tea and biscuits stage.

TOMMY: That was a grand dinner, Nora love. Wasn't it, daughters?

AINE: It was, Daddy. Lovely.

BRID: Oh, there's nobody can grill chops and boil spuds the way my mother does.

Exchange of looks — pause.

NORA: More tea anybody? Tommy?

TOMMY: Sorry, Nora?

NORA: Tea, Tommy! Tea!

TOMMY: No thanks, Nora. But I'll have a wee drop of that coffee that the girls are drinking.

NORA: Oh, you will, will you?

TOMMY: It smells quare and good.

NORA: Does it now? And I suppose you'll be going to Brazil for your holidays, Tommy Murphy! Or will it be Kenya this year?

TOMMY: What's that, Nora? Sure you know we don't go on holidays. . .

NORA: Hmmm! Do I know that alright!

TOMMY: Day trips is what I like. Whitehead. Newcastle. Somewhere not too far. And you can return to your own bed of a night.

AINE: Do you remember, Brid, going away for the day as kids? God, the excitement of it. Blue skies. Not so sandy beaches.

BRID: Buckets and spades. Whirligigs. Candy floss. Hard boiled eggs.

AINE: I loved Whitehead. And Browns Bay!

BRID: And Bangor!

TOMMY: Bangor? Jesus, I always hated the sight of Bangor. A right black hole was yon place. Sure you couldn't go near the place during the months of July and August but there wouldn't always be one of *their* Masonic bloody Lodges marching up and down on the sea front. Pickie Pool wouldn't have held enough water to drown the bastards. Bangor? Orange men and the Sally Army gadging money. That was Bangor!

NORA: And to think that that's thirty years ago and more. Have things changed at all? Still, it was a bit of colour for the kids. Sure, when they were wee, they loved to watch the men marching and the bands playing. Our Brid rhymed to be a majorette for weeks one time. . .

TOMMY: And weren't we the right bloody eejits stood with them, Nora? But then, Catholics in the fifties took all that nonsense. Think what it might have done to our daughters' minds, Nora! All that orange and red white and blue.

NORA: They both *look* like it harmed them right enough, Tommy. Like yourself, they're forever singing 'The Sash'.

Aine and Brid sing 'The Sash my father wore.' Tommy enraged.

TOMMY: That's enough! If you want to sing the likes of that, get back to England . . . NOW!

NORA: Tommy, what's wrong with you? Sure it's only a cod we're having?

TOMMY: There's no codding, Nora, about that. And those Loyalist bastards weren't codding when they sprayed those men in the Avenue Bar. And you can be sure it was 'The Sash' they were singing up the Shankill when they were drinking and crowing about it afterward. Jesus, is there to be no end to what we Taigs have to take from them? And you can be bloody sure, Mrs Thatcher won't be standing in mournful black out of respect to any dead Catholics. Christ, if I was a young man today, I'm telling you now, Colonel Gadaffi couldn't keep me supplied with enough arms and ammunition for I'd soon come to an agreement with them alright. But it wouldn't be at Hillsboro' I'd sign it — it would be down at the docks, with them loading their possessions onto boats! We must respect the two traditions? How the hell can you respect something that's wrong? And they're wrong and they know they're wrong and everybody in the bloody universe knows they're wrong, but since when was it wrong to be wrong? Sure the whole world's gone mad altogether. . .

Tommy stops short. Notices three women staring at him.

TOMMY: What are yiz all looking at me like that for?

Pause.
Nora and daughters convulse in laughter.
Light change, music and sound.

3 | SCENE

Murphy girls' bedroom. Aine and Brid prepare for bed.

AINE: Do you ever think of coming back, Brid?

BRID: What? To Belfast? To live?

AINE: Aye.

BRID: Sometimes. But you know, Aine, I don't think it's ever possible to go back once you've left. You've gone. Especially now that I've been away such a long time. Belfast isn't part of me anymore. That's not to say I'm part of London. I'm an outsider there too. Being Irish you're always an outsider in England — even in multi-racial, cosmopolitan London. And I think the Irish are less accepted there than other 'ethnic' groups. It's not surprising — we are seen to be part of the 'at war' team — but sure I'm an outsider here too. The Irish don't forgive those who left. Though they'll claim you as one of their own if you make good. Besides, the Belfast I was a part of, the Belfast I still love, doesn't exist anymore. My Belfast is the Belfast of my childhood and youth. . .

AINE: Do you ever regret leaving, Brid?

BRID: No, Aine. I don't. I may have lost something by leaving, but I think on balance I gained a lot more. . .

AINE: What did you gain?

Pause.

BRID: A kind of freedom. . .

AINE: But you've just said you're an outsider in London . . . you're not accepted. . .

BRID: But that in itself is a sort of freedom. There's no ties — no pull — no expectations. If I was English, I can see it in John, there's a pull to be something. To do something. To be involved. I'm not saying I'm not involved. Of course I'm involved by being there. But there's no one making any real demands on me like there would be if I was here in Ireland. A kind of calling you to task all the time — politically — religiously. Like even at home here with Mother and Father — 'no word of you getting married yet?' People always pressurizing you to conform to their values. And it's hard to constantly fight that in a narrow, provincial society like Northern Ireland. There's a lot to be said for the uncaring anonymity of the big metropolis. I mean, how do you cope, Aine?

AINE: Me?

BRID: You're right bang smack in the middle of it, teaching in the convent school we used to attend. Don't you find it restricting? Don't you ever feel like telling the Mother Peters of this world to fuck away off and leave you alone?

AINE: I did. Once. But I'm going to be forty this year, Brid, and as time passes, there are battles I once would have fought I don't see as battles anymore. Now that may sound like packing in the game to you but age, if you like, has given me a different perspective on things. I don't expect immediate results anymore. Life trundles on regardless of upheavals, personal tragedies, political tragedies, deaths. Nobody living here through the last twenty years of our troubles could anymore expect changes overnight. You and I once did, Brid. We all did twenty years ago — we thought then that the revolution was just around the corner and that Ireland was going to be transformed miraculously into a 20th century ideal workers' and small farmers' republic. . . But Jesus, look at it . . . the very idea of such a hope, such an ideal, such a belief, sounds like an insanity in the face of how things really are. If anything, Ireland is more conservative now than it was 20 years ago. . .

BRID: So, why do you stay, Aine?

AINE: Why do I stay? Probably fear, Brid.

BRID: Fear? Of what?

AINE: Fear of leaving. Fear of the unknown. I suppose, you could say, better the ghetto you know than the big world you don't. Where would I go to? London?

BRID: Why not?

AINE: Nah. I don't fancy it, Brid. And sure I can live under Mrs Thatcher here, I don't have to go to London for that. No, you see, Brid, you made the move when there was still hope. I stayed and I've got stuck.

BRID: Is it Mother and Father that keeps you? For you know what's going to happen if you're not careful. . .

AINE: You mean, when one of them dies, I'll be left, in traditional fashion, to look after the other?

BRID: Exactly.

AINE: If it happens, it happens that way. And I don't really mind, Brid. My mother needs somebody around. She'd go demented if there was just her and my father. He's not an easy man to live with.

BRID: He never was.

AINE: And he's got worse, Brid. We can talk about lost hopes. That what's happening today is a far cry from our civil rights and Peoples Democracy days, but maybe it's even harder for him. What about his hopes and his ambitions for us, his daughters? It's what he lived for, after all, and maybe we haven't measured up to his expectations.

BRID: Daughters never do, Aine. And it strikes me that the first fault of parents is to live for their offspring instead of living for themselves.

AINE: And if they had 'lived for themselves' would we be where we are today?

BRID: And where *is* that, Aine? Where exactly are we today? It's not where we twenty years ago thought we'd be, is it?

AINE: Twenty years ago! I was at Queens. You had just finished at St Dominic's. Do you remember that summer, Brid?

BRID: Hitch-hiking round Ireland. Mayo. Sligo. Galway. Dublin.

AINE: Do you remember the Dutch students we met in Galway?

BRID: Aye, I certainly do. They were gorgeous. And I remember if it hadn't been for that holy Joe that ran the youth hostel, you and I might have lost our virginity a lot earlier than we did. 'Ah now lads, you're as welcome here as anybody but I don't think it's right and proper that you should be entertaining these young Irish girls in your room at this hour!'

AINE: They were gone the next morning. Our Amsterdam lovers that never were.

BRID: You know, you and I were in bad form for the rest of that trip. Sexually thwarted, we'd been. Weren't we right bloody eejits to let yon Conemara puritan stop us from enjoying ourselves? Students throughout Europe were ripping up paving stones and dancing naked in the streets. . .

AINE: While we were having our virtues preserved on the West Coast of Ireland.

BRID: But you know, Aine. . . It was like the last summer of innocence. The summer after that was the summer of '69 — the summer the British Army arrived. . .

Light change — music.
Enter soldier in battle dress with rifle, bayonet drawn, as if into bedroom. Hold music loud.
Blackout.

4 SCENE

Murphy kitchen. Caitlin Murphy with Pram.

CAITLIN: Hello! Anybody home? Anybody up yet? Hello. Mother! Aine, Brid!

Enter Brid in dressing gown.

BRID: Good morning, Caitlin.

CAITLIN: Good *morning*? Do you know what time it is, Brid Murphy? It's nearly noon-time. Christ, you haven't changed. Still as fond of your bed as ever. . .

They embrace.

BRID: Good to see you, little sister.

CAITLIN: Well, I'll not say you're looking well — for you're not. You look like you're just up after a hard night with a sex fiend. This is Belfast, you know. People get up early here. Most of us have been out banging bin-lids and throwing stones since before dawn. Will I make coffee? Black coffee? You look like you need rejuvenation of some kind.

BRID: Yes. Please. That would be very nice.

Coffee business.

CAITLIN: Well, big sister, how are you doing? And what brings you to the emerald isle this time? Are you on holiday or just home for a funeral? The way you're looking it could be your own. And why didn't you bring that nice English man you're living with with you? What's wrong with us? You ashamed, Brid Murphy, of your working class Irish

Catholic origins? Or is he afraid to come? Afraid of getting shot by one of his fellow countrymen?

Exchange of looks.

CAITLIN: It's alright. It's alright. I'm only joking. Relax. I don't believe in talking about politics or religion. Now, babies. And children. I can talk about them until I bore myself.

BRID: Congratulations.

CAITLIN: Oh so my Mother told you. And what *do* you think it'll be this time? A boy or a girl?

BRID: I hope a girl. What do you want yourself?

CAITLIN: Me? I'm not sure I want it at all.

BRID: Why have it then?

CAITLIN: Now, look here, sister from foreign parts. Don't you come back here to Ireland with any of your alien ideologies or foreignisms. This is Catholic Ireland! . . . We cherish our children here. We produce babies. It's the only thing we do produce. Babies and dead people! Besides, do you realize that by suggesting 'abortion', you have fallen under the influence of Protestantism which is out to stop us Catholics from producing Fenian babies for fear that, instead of bombing our loyalist friends into a Catholic Republic, we will outbreed them and smother them with the huge breasts of the Moving Statues of Our Lady!

The sisters laugh together.

BRID: Caitlin, where the hell do you get all your energy from?

CAITLIN: Having babies, sister. It keeps the hormones and juices bubbling. *I* don't need *black* coffee in the mornings to waken me. You know why? Because I have two sons who have no sense of time and who do not recognize the distinction between day and night — light and dark. They are animals who crave food and attention at all times. And they have turned me into an animal who recognizes no barriers of time or space. They cry. I jump. They jump. I cry. Now, for Christ's sake, knock that coffee into you. Get washed and dressed for we're heading into Belfast Town and there you will have the supreme pleasure of participating in Irish Catholic family life by examining closely the new 1–3 year old romper suits in the kiddies department of M & S, British Home Stores and C & A — those renowned and great bastions of the Irish retail trade. Up the Republic! Come, sister, shift yourself. We are going on a long journey. In a Peoples' taxi!

Baby in pram starts crying.

CAITLIN: Shut your mouth, you Fenian monster!

Blackout. Music and sound.

5   SCENE

This surreal monologue scene is Brid travelling in a black taxi down the Falls Road. Sights of buildings prompt her memory to speak. Special lighting effects. Sounds and music.

BRID: St Agnes Church. 1965. Father White. And where did he kiss, you my child? On the lips, Father. And then? He touched my body, Father. I see. Did he touch you above or below the waist, my child. Above. And below Father. I see. You know, my child, it is a sin of impurity to allow a boy to touch any part of your body? Yes, Father. Boys find it harder to control themselves than girls, my child, which is why you should avoid occasions of sin. You know what occasions of sin are, don't you, my child? No, Father. Occasions of sin are when you are alone with a boy in a quiet place. Down a lane. In a car. Under a tree in a park. Do you understand, my child? Yes, Father. You seem an intelligent good girl. So, remember this. Boys are beasts. And you, the girl, must control them. You must always avoid occasions of sin. But if you should, through weakness, find yourself in such an occasion of sin, remember it is your duty to say no to any impure suggestions or acts by the boy. For you have the responsibility for two souls. Your own. And the boy's. Sinning yourself is bad enough and punishable by God, but to lead another into sin can lead to damnation in hell for ever and ever. You understand, my child? Yes, Father. And remember — this boy who committed these impure acts with you, you must never see him again. But, Father? Yes, my child? I'm meeting him behind the Church after Confession.

Sound and music.

Casement Park. 1966. 50th Anniversary of Easter Rising. 1916. Seven Men. Seven Days. Pageant. Flags. Tricolour. Green. White. Orange. Starry Plough. Blue. Yellow. Gaelic footballers. Hurlers. Dancers. Celtic costumes. Celtic crosses. Music. Bands. People cheering. Loudspeaker. Names. Patrick Pearse. Thomas Clarke. Thomas McDonagh. Sean McDermott. Eamonn Ceannt. Joseph Plunkett. James Connolly. Seven Men. Seven Days.

Sound and music.

Andersonstown Police Station. 1969. Civil Rights March. Parading down Falls Road. Stop outside police station opposite Milltown Cemetery. Marchers' chant. One Man, One Vote. Sing. Loudly. Powerfully. We Shall Overcome. We shall overcome. Few youths throw stones. Local solicitor pleads for calm. This is a peaceful march. A peaceful demonstration. There will be no throwing stones. March on, he said. Frightened faces at window of barracks. One Man. One Vote. Andersonstown Barracks. Today. An Army fortress. High walls. Corrugated iron. Concrete. Electronic equipment. No marching. No chanting. No singing. Only the dead asleep in Milltown Cemetery.

Sound and music.

Dominican Convent. St Dominic's High School for Girls. 1961–1968. Nuns! Black and white habit. Clatter of huge rosary beads tied round waist as they strode through corridors. Prefects. Order. Did they prefer the daughters of publicans and doctors? Snobs. You used to have to

have a dowry to enter the Dominican Order. Married to
God. Brides of Christ. How many women did God have?
Sexual guilt. The girl must always be in control. The nuns
said it. Father White said it. It must be true? Sneaking
admiration for them. Clever women. Independence of a
sort. Do you think you might have a vocation, Brid
Murphy? A vocation, Sister? Me? A nun? But I don't
believe in God, Sister. We all have doubts sometimes,
Brid. Pray to Our Lady. I don't want to pray to Our Lady.
St Dominic, then. I don't want to pray to him either. I
don't pray, Sister. I'm an atheist. I'm thinking of
becoming a Communist. Sister. Sister, are you alright?
You may think you're an atheist, Brid Murphy — you may
even become a Communist. But you'll still always be a
Dominican girl . . . a Dominican girl . . . a Dominican
girl. . .

Sound and music.

Leeson Street. August '69. British Army marching up
Falls Road. Bayonets drawn. Sean McManus standing at
street corner watching English soldiers. *Dia duit, Sean.*
Dia is Muire duit, Brid. The nerve in Sean's right cheek
throbbing. Pulsating with anger. Hatred. Frustration. His
ancient enemy on Irish soil. Again. It's now five years
since Sean McManus died at the hands of his ancient
enemy. *Dia duit, Sean.* . .

Sound and music.

St Mary's Irish Christian Brothers Grammar School.
Barrack Street.

Boys! Boys! Boys!
Sound and music.

BRID: Marquee Dance Hall. 1968. Sunday night hop. Hot.
Sweaty. Flashing lights. Long-haired group. Lead singer
thinks he's Mick Jagger. 'I can' get no satisfaction'.
Standing around. Waiting. Sitting around. Waiting.
Here's one now. He's giving me the once over. Twice
over. Thrice over. How many times does he have to
visually measure me before he asks me to dance? Clammy
hands. Smell of cigarette smoke. After-shave. Smoochy
number. His arms round my waist. My arms round his

neck. Closer. Closer. His thigh against my thigh. Back
and forth. Side to side. Closer. Closer. Is that his. . .?
Fear. Desire. Frustration. The girl must always be in
control. 'Can I leave you home? I have my brother's car
for the night.' You know what occasions of sin are, don't
you, my child. Occasions of sin. Occasions of sin. 'I'm
with my sister.' 'Oh, I see. Thanks for the dance.' Thanks.
Flashing lights. Long-haired group. Marquee Dance Hall.
1968. 'I can' get no satisfaction'.

Sound and music

CAITLIN: Brid! Brid! Have you any change for the taxi? I only
have a tenner. Brid! Where were you anyhow? God, it
was always the same going out with you — half the time
you end up talking to yourself. What the hell do you be
thinking about anyway? I swear to God, those Dominican
nuns turned your head with all that education!

Light change — sound of babies crying.
Lighting to produce speeded-up film effect.
Caitlin and Brid frantically shopping and pushing buggy —
this to be worked out in rehearsal/improvisation.
Light change.
Caitlin and Brid sit in café exhausted. Sipping coffee.
Surrounded by buggy and an inordinate number of
shopping bags from M & S, BHS, C & A, etc.
Silence.

BRID: Caitlin?

CAITLIN: Yes, Brid?

BRID: Are you happy?

CAITLIN: Happy? Happy? Who the hell have you ever met was
happy?

BRID: Nobody.

CAITLIN: See. You're not put in this world to be happy, sister.
I'm not sure why we're put in this world, but I do know
happiness is not necessarily part of the plan. A vale of
tears and suffering more like. Still, it's never dull here. I
mean there's always a funeral to go to. You know, the
clergy must be making a fortune signing Mass cards. And
then getting another fiver or tenner slipped to them to say

Masses for the repose of all those souls in Milltown Cemetery. Peace? Peace is the last bloody thing the Catholic Church wants here. Bad for business, peace. Talk about racketeeering and protection money, I bet you even the Black Taxis are being operated from the Vatican!

Laughter.

BRID: Do you like being married, sister?

CAITLIN: Brid, love, nobody *likes* being married. Being married is one of those states in life that you cope with — it has nothing to do with likes or dislikes.

BRID: Don't you love your husband, Sean Doyle?

CAITLIN: Living with a man is one of the most difficult occupations a woman can undertake, Brid. But what am I telling you for? Maybe 'Englishmen' are different. But Irish men — Catholic Irish men — worship at three shrines. At the breasts of their mothers, at the altar of Christ's mother and at the bottomless pit of Cathleen Ni Houlihan. Tell me, what hope has an ordinary girl against legend, religion and mythology?

BRID: What about motherhood?

CAITLIN: I thrive on it. It's the ultimate natural experience. Shitty bums and gumless mouths gnawing at your tits. Go on, ask me another, big sister. . .

BRID: Whatever happened. . .?

CAITLIN: To the Murphy Girls?

Music/sound.

Murphy home. Nora Murphy is reading 'The Deaths' in the Irish News Newspaper. Tommy is dozing on armchair. Pause.

NORA: Tommy. Listen to this. 'McQuillan, Francis. Peacefully at his home. Beloved husband of Bridget. Sacred heart of Jesus have mercy on his soul. Funeral on Monday after 10 o'clock Mass at St Theresa's Church to Hannahstown Cemetery. Deeply regretted by his wife, son, daughter-in-law and grandchildren.' That must be the McQuillan that was a friend of your father's. Wasn't it Francis McQuillan was on the run with your father at the time of the Black and Tans? You should go to that funeral, Tommy. God, isn't that sad? He must've been brave and old though. He musta been nearly ninety or more for sure, wasn't your father 84 when he died and that's what — eight, nine years ago. God, these aul ones last well, don't they? I'm sure I'll not last so long. You might do, Tommy. You're a Murphy. Even if you only lasted as long as your father you still have another 20 years. So, will you go to the funeral, Tommy?

Tommy snores.

NORA: Jesus, Mary and Holy Saint Joseph, have you not been listening to me at all?

TOMMY: What's that Nora? What were you saying? Did I hear you mention a funeral? Who's dead?

NORA: Christ, is it any wonder you Murphys last so long for youse are a dab hand at looking after yourselves. No. It's alright, Tommy. Relax. Go back to sleep.

TOMMY: Sure, you've woken me now. Who's dead? Did you say somebody was dead?

NORA: It's yourself was acting it. Francis McQuillan, I said, was dead.

TOMMY: Who?

NORA: Francis McQuillan. Friend of your father's.

TOMMY: Francis McQuillan? He was no friend of my father's.

NORA: I thought your father and him were on the run together.

TOMMY: Who told you that, Nora?

NORA: You did, Tommy Murphy.

TOMMY: Did I? When?

NORA: Jesus! Years ago. When we first got married. And you were bumming about your rebel Republican background.

TOMMY: I don't remember telling you anything of the sort.

NORA: Francis McQuillan wasn't 'on the run' with your father then? Was your father *ever* 'on the run'? I know he was good at running to the pub and the bookies and to the football and to the boxing but that's not what 'on the run' is supposed to mean, is it?

TOMMY: Nora. Why are you suddenly attacking my father? The man's dead. You're not supposed to speak ill of the dead.

NORA: I wasn't attacking your father.

TOMMY: Well, why did you just say he was always running to the pub and the bookies and football and boxing. . .

NORA: Well, so he was. . .

TOMMY: There you go again with your attack on my father. . .

NORA: What's wrong with you, Tommy? It used to be you never had a good word to say about your own father. Sure for years I couldn't get you to go to see him.

TOMMY: Because you didn't want me to go and see him. Because the Murphys, you thought, were snobs.

NORA: So they were. They thought they were somebody because they owned a bit of land here and there. But sure there's no use owning land if there's nobody to work it. Selling it and drinking the money was more in their line. But sure, that's the Irish all over. . .

TOMMY: Nora. You've now moved from attacking my father, to castigating the Murphy clan to slurring the entire Irish nation. . .

NORA: Is it any wonder, sleeping as they do. You know, I sometimes think that if Maggie Thatcher declared in the morning that she was abolishing the border, half the dozing country wouldn't even realize. And would it make any real difference to them if they did know?

TOMMY: Nora, love, what's wrong with you the night?

NORA: What do you mean, Tommy Murphy, what's wrong with me? There's nothing wrong with me. And don't give me any of that aul 'Nora, love' stuff in that phoney concerned voice of yours. Go back to sleep, Tommy. I'll read the death notices on my own!

Enter Caitlin.

CAITLIN: There's nothing like married life is there? I was just saying the same thing to my husband there now before I left the house. Delighted he was at the thought of me going out for the evening and him having to mind *his sons*. 'How long's your sister staying?' says he: 'Does this mean you'll be out every night she's here?' says he. 'What time will you be back?' says he. 'If the boys wake what will I do with them?' says he. 'Murder them,' says I. 'But don't make a mess and if you do, have it cleaned up before I come back.' And you know what he says to me — 'Where do you keep the hoover?'

Nora laughs heartily. Puts newspaper aside. Tommy looks over the top of the Republican News and smiles.

NORA: And how are my grandsons, Caitlin?

CAITLIN: They were alive and sleeping when I left, Mother, but who knows?

NORA: Oh, don't you kid yourself, my girl, you're a lucky woman has a husband like Sean Doyle who's so good in the house. In my day, things were very different. We didn't have hoovers and fridges and disposable nappies or husbands prepared to sit in of a night to let their womenfolk out for a wee jaunt.

Tommy shifts awkwardly.

Enter Brid and Aine from upstairs.

CAITLIN: Oh, there's you are! It is the night you two girls are going out, isn't it? Jesus, would you look at the style from the Big Smoke! It's a drinking club on the Falls Road you're going to, Brid, not the West End. And Lord, the Aine one's nearly as bad. Is that the style these days in the Dominican staff-room? Still, I suppose you single girls have to flaunt it a bit for anybody to take any notice!

BRID: Does looking attractive stop after marriage, Caitlin?

AINE: I'm not going out if you two are going to start bickering at each other all bloody night.

CAITLIN: Are the Murphy Girls ready for the road?

AINE: Are you sure youse won't come with us? Mammy? Daddy?

NORA: No. No. Away yiz go. That aul club gets awful noisy and smokey on a Friday night. Mind yourselves now. Yiz won't be too late?

TOMMY: And if the army and the R.U.C. raid it, don't take any nonsense from them. Youse know your rights. Remember. Youse are Murphys!

NORA: Saints preserve us, would you listen to the clan chieftain. Away there, Tommy, and put the kettle on and you and me'll have a wee hot Jameson. And then you can tell me all about the great rebels the Murphys were in the days of the Celtic mists.

Nora winks at her daughters.
Hold and blackout.
Music and sound.

7 SCENE

Gaelic Club. Aine, Brid, and Caitlin sitting at table with drinks. Music stops.

MAN ON MICROPHONE: *A Cairde.* Some of you will have noticed that sitting amongst us tonight are three beautiful women — there's more than three beautiful women here of course — but the three I'm referring to are three sisters. The three daughters of our old comrade Tommy Murphy and his good wife, Nora. We know Caitlin Murphy well, or Mrs Sean Doyle as she is these days, for Sean has been a supporter and member of this club for many years. We know Aine Murphy and so do many of our own daughters for she has been an inspiration to them in their study of 'English' literature at St Dominic's school here on the Falls Road. And some of us will remember well the third daughter, not often seen amongst us these days but tonight it's great to have her with us, home on holiday, I understand, from London — Brid Murphy, who for many years ran Irish classes here in this very club. And in those early days almost twenty years ago, before our current 'troubles' even started, Brid enlivened manys an *Oice Ceol* with her rendering of songs in the Irish. So, *a cairde*, I'm going to take the liberty of asking Brid Murphy to come up now, if she would, and, as in those nights of long ago, give us a song! Ladies and gentlemen, Brid Murphy.

BRID: What would happen if I refused? Just sat here and smiled and ignored that big sentimental fool?

CAITLIN: We'd all probably get knee-capped. Get up there, sister, and sing.

AINE: Pretend you're doing it just for us, Brid.

BRID: Well, I can tell you now, I'm certainly not doing it for yon eejit. Deliver us always now and at the hour of our death from the Gaelgoiri of Ireland.

CAITLIN: Sing 'Donal Og'. Go on. Get up there. The sooner you sing, the sooner I'll buy you another drink.

Brid approaches platform and the man with the microphone. She sings song in Irish. Applause. Returns to sisters.

CAITLIN: God, if only your London friends could see you now. Brid Murphy the toast of the Falls Road Irish speakers.

AINE: Your voice hasn't changed, Brid.

BRID: No. Not since I had the operation.

CAITLIN: There's men in here would have their balls off to be able to sing like that.

BRID: There's a brave few of them looks that they've had anyway.

CAITLIN: Hey, girl. That's our Irish manhood you're talking about. . .

AINE: Talking of which. . .

Enter Pat O'Brien.

PAT: Brid?

BRID: Yes?

PAT: You don't recognize me?

BRID: Should I?

PAT: Pat O'Brien.

Brid almost chokes.

BRID: Pat O'Brien from the Glen Road? You're joking me?

PAT: No. It's me alright. The same one.

BRID: What happened to you?

PAT: Have I changed so much? You're just the same.

BRID: That's a lie and you know it. What happened to your hair?

Pat runs a hand over his balding head and shrugs.

AINE: Don't be so ignorant, Brid.

CAITLIN: Nothing, if not forthright, our sister. I'm Caitlin. How do you do, Pat. Is it true what they say about bald men?

PAT: And what's that?

CAITLIN: That they're very sexy. . .

AINE: Would you like to join us, Pat?

PAT: You don't mind? Let me get youse a drink first. What's it to be? Brid?

BRID: Gin and tonic, please.

CAITLIN: Vodka and lemonade.

AINE: The same. Vodka. Thank you.

PAT: I won't be a second.

CAIRLIN: Aine? Is that the Pat O'Brien that's not long out of the Kesh?

AINE: Now, how would I know that, Caitlin?

CAITLIN: I thought teachers at the Dominican Convent knew everything even before it happened. The nuns certainly do.

AINE: What I do know is that once upon a time, and you, Caitlin, were probably too young to realize, but our sister here had a quare notion of Mr O'Brien and he of her. . .

Pat returns with drinks.

PAT: Here y'are then. Two vodkas. And a gin and tonic for you, Brid.

CAITLIN: You'd know she lived in England, Pat, wouldn't you . . . drinking gin and tonic?

BRID: And you're from the Russian steppes, I suppose, Smirnoff features.

AINE: *Slainte*, everyone.

PAT: *Slainte!*

Silence.

PAT: When I heard you singing, Brid, I thought I couldn't not say hello to you. You still sing as well as you did too.

BRID: Thank you. But my voice like my face has also changed. Twenty years is a long time, Pat.

PAT: Is it twenty years since I last saw you?

BRID: Near enough. We were young then. And you still had all your hair.

PAT: You're living in London now?

BRID: Yes.

PAT: Working?

BRID: I'm a teacher.

PAT: You're joking!

CAITLIN: Her pupils think it's a joke as well.

PAT: So, you ended up doing what you swore you'd never do.

BRID: You remember me saying that?

PAT: I certainly do. You used to make such a song and dance about it when I teased you.

BRID: Aine's a teacher too.

PAT: Yes. I heard the *'fear a ti'* say you taught English at St Dominic's. I think my sister's girls were in your class sometime. McNulty's their name. Grainne. And Sinead.

AINE: I know them. Yes.

CAITLIN: I'm not a teacher, Pat. You'll be glad to hear. I'm only a mother and wife. . .

PAT: You're Sean Doyle's wife, aren't you?

CAITLIN: You know my Sean?

PAT: Sean and I used to be in the same *cumann*.

CAITLIN: Before he was married that was. My Sean hasn't been involved.

PAT: Yeh. I suppose it was. It's a brave clatter of years ago. It was a long time, I know, before I went into the Kesh.

BRID: How long were you in for, Pat?

PAT: Twelve years.

BRID: A long time out of one life.

PAT: It seemed longer at the time.

BRID: And now?

PAT: This and that. . .

CAITLIN: Are you married, Pat?

PAT: No. I never seemed to have the time to get round to that.

BRID: Are you still living with your mother on the Glen Road?

PAT: Still there.

BRID: How is she?

PAT: Getting old. But not bad. Her spirit's great. But she can't get around like she did. What about you, Brid? Are you married?

BRID: Not married exactly. . .

CAITLIN: She lives in sin with an Englishman.

AINE: Knock that vodka into you, Caitlin. Your husband and two sons will be wondering if you've deserted them.

CAITLIN: What's your hurry? I'm enjoying myself.

AINE: And all pleasure must come to an end. Come along, little sister. I'll walk you home.

PAT: Youse going now? What about another drink?

AINE: No thank you, Pat. We really must go. You don't have to rush, Brid. You're on holiday after all. Right, Caitlin, get your coat on. Nice meeting you, Pat. All the best.

CAITLIN: I'll tell my Sean I was talking to you.

PAT: Yes. Right. Say hello to him for me. He was a good comrade, was Sean.

CAITLIN: See you later, Brid. . .

Exit Aine and Caitlin.
Pause.

BRID: My turn this time. Bottle of Guinness?

PAT: Please. Thanks.

Brid gets up. Light change to 1968 dance hall — music.
Brid dancing twist.
Pat approaches Brid. Nods. They dance.
Music stops.

PAT: You stayin' up for the next dance?

BRID: Are you askin'?

Music. A slow number from that year.

PAT: Do you come here often?

BRID: The Sunday night hop most weeks. Do you?

PAT: The same.

Pause.

PAT: Are you still at school?

BRID: I'm in the upper sixth. I leave in June.

PAT: St Dominic's?

BRID: How d'you know?

PAT: You can tell.

BRID: Are you at the Christian Brothers?

PAT: No. The Tech. I got thrown out of the Christian Brothers.

BRID: Why? Did you fail your 'A' levels?

PAT: How d'you know?

BRID: You can tell.

Pause.

PAT: Whereabouts do you live?

BRID: Andersonstown.

PAT: So do I.

> *Pause.*

BRID: Have you got a car?

PAT: No. But I might be able to get you a lift home. A friend of my brother's has his father's car for the night.

BRID: I usually get a taxi with my sister.

PAT: Is she here the night?

BRID: Why do you ask?

PAT: Nothing. I was just wondering.

> *Pause.*

BRID: She's with her boyfriend.

PAT: Who is?

BRID: My sister. That's her over there.

> *Waves to sister.*

VOICE: Thank you very much boys and girls. Your next dance please.

> *Music stops. Brid and Pat disengage.*

BRID: Thanks for the dance.

PAT: Do you fancy a coke?

BRID: Alright.

PAT: You better take my hand. It's a bit crowded.

BRID: Afraid of losing me?

> *They smile at each other. Hold.*
> *Light change to 1969 sound; music and radio bulletin.*
> *Mimed participation in riot — stylized.*
> *Beatles — 'Revolution'.*

SCENE 8

In the street. Pat O'Brien and Brid dander along.

BRID: So you're still involved, Pat?

PAT: Politically? Oh aye. The war goes on, Brid.

BRID: The war goes on. . . And for how long, Pat?

Pat shrugs.

BRID: And who's going to win the war?

PAT: We will. Eventually. Isn't that what your Ken Livingstone said?

BRID: And he must know?

PAT: He's the only politician, Irish or English, that didn't preach self righteously after Enniskillen, Brid. He's done a lot for us, y'know.

BRID: Unlike your own Irish Catholic clergy who couldn't wait to issue moral encylicals against youse.

PAT: So, what's new about that, Brid?

BRID: Nothing, Pat. Nothing. But do you never sometimes stop to think that the biggest enemy of Ireland is not the Brits but the Holy Roman Catholic and Apostolic Church? The Brits may occupy the land but the Roman Church occupies the minds of the people. It's easier to shift soldiers over land than it is to expel incense from the brain.

PAT: You're talking like a Protestant, Brid. Rome Rule, is it?

BRID: It is. Rome Rule. And the Protestants are right. Who can blame them for not wanting to live in a Catholic State? For that's what the South is, Pat. A green, reactionary Catholic State. An 'anti-Republican' State. Wolfe Tone, the father of Irish Republicanism, was no friend of Rome or any religion. He wanted to take Ireland away from her superstitions towards enlightenment.

PAT: Let us get rid of the Brits first. And then we can let the people decide what the nature of the new state should be.

BRID: Let the people decide, is it? But even if they were asked, Pat, we know what the people would decide and your Movement, I think, would do nothing to counter it. Twenty years ago we were for revolution and socialism, not for simply removing the border and having the Cardinal elected as Taoiseach and the Dail moved up to Armagh.

PAT: These things take time, Brid. Ireland *is* a Catholic country. Change doesn't happen as fast as we thought it would, twenty years ago. . .

BRID: But I'm running out of time, Pat O'Brien. The years are dropping off me like the hair on your head. The war has become an eternal siege and I don't see the gates of hope ever opening. Rome has got not only the revolution but the country by the balls.

PAT: Like Maggie Thatcher has your precious England. . .

BRID: But even Maggie Thatcher will pass. Rome seems to go on for fuckin' ever. . .

Silence.

BRID: Do you resent people like me who left?

PAT: I do when they come back and complain that we haven't achieved what they wanted — having made no attempt to stay and fight themselves.

BRID: (*to herself*) Once you've left, you can never go back.

PAT: The likes of you, Brid, walked out on the revolution. So there's no point in coming home now to gripe that the revolution hasn't occurred. Stay away, if you don't like what you see. Go back to London. Live in 'free' England.

BRID: Would you like to go to bed with me, Pat?

PAT: What?

BRID: I just thought because we didn't go 'all the way' twenty years ago, we could do so now!

PAT: Are you having me on?

BRID: I will if we can go back to your mother's and do it. . .

PAT: But that's impossible. My mother. . .

BRID: *Mother* Church got you by the balls as well, Pat?

Sound of car moving very fast.

PAT: Look out! Get down, Brid. . .

Pat dives on Brid, pulling her to ground. Sound of gunfire and a car driving off.
Blackout.

SCENE | 9

Sound of ambulance siren. Special lighting effect. Blue light flashing. Cut sound. Light keeps flashing throughout scene.

BRID: Midnight. West Belfast. Andersonstown Road. Walking home with old flame. Arguing. Politics and religion. 'Mother Church got you by the balls, Pat O'Brien?' Sound of car. Get down, Brid. Old flame jumps on top of me. Fall to the ground. Sound of gunfire. Nothing. Then pain. Pain in left arm. Right hand. Wet. Is that blood? My blood? Dark. Can't see. Wince with pain. Old flame lying beside me. Don't move yet, Brid. Car has gone. Are you alright? I think I've been shot, Pat. Jesus! No! My arm, Pat. My arm hurts like hell. Lie still. I'll get an ambulance. Pat disappears. Silence. Darkness. Rain begins to fall. Alone. Lying alone. On the Andytown Road. Shot. I've been shot! But I'm only visitin'. Home on holiday. Why me? Footsteps. I hear footsteps. 'Ambulance be here soon. Bloody man wasn't going to let me use his phone. Good Samaritan, eh? How do you feel?' Sick. 'You'll be alright. I can't see properly but it's only a flesh wound, I think. You'll be alright when you get to hospital, Brid. I can't go with you. You understand. Too many questions. Police. Army. You know the score. Here's the ambulance now'.

Sound of ambulance in distance. Coming closer.

'I'll head off. You'll be alright. I'll ring later to see how you are. Right. All the best. Sorry.' Footsteps. Running. Alone again. Sound of ambulance. Flashing blue light. Flashing blue light. Flashing blue . . . flashing. . .

Sound of ambulance siren loud, then cut.
Light change.

10 | SCENE

Hospital ward. Brid sitting up in bed. Arm in sling. A young R.U.C. policewoman sitting on chair next to bed. Silence.

BRID: Can I ask you something, Constable?

Policewoman looks awkward and nervous.

BRID: What age are you?

P/W: Twenty, nearly twenty one.

BRID: You were born in 1968?

P/W: August 9th.

BRID: (*almost to herself*) You were three years of age on the day they introduced internment. August 9th 1971.

Policewoman half smiles. Pause.

BRID: What made you join the R.U.C., Constable?

Pause.

P/W: Well, there's not much work in Northern Ireland and my parents thought it might be a career for me.

BRID: And what do you think? *Do* you think it's a 'career'?

Pause.

P/W: Sometimes. At least it's steady.

BRID: A steady career?

P/W: Do you mind if I ask you something?

BRID: Not at all.

P/W: You live in London, don't you? The nurse told me.

BRID: Yes. I live in London.

P/W: What's it like?

BRID: A city. . .

P/W: I'd like to go to London. Me and my friend are thinking of going for a holiday. The shops are great, I hear, and there's loads of clubs and discos. Do you ever go to the West End?

Brid smiles and nods.

P/W: Is it true they don't like Irish people over there?

BRID: Some people don't. Sometimes.

P/W: I have another friend. She's been to London but she said the English people kept saying pardon to her. She thought they were being very polite then she realized they didn't understand what she was saying — our accent, I suppose.

BRID: Do you consider yourself Irish then, Constable?

P/W: Well, I don't have an English accent. I have an Irish accent. But I'm British.

P/W smiles shyly. Brid returns smile.
Pause.

P/W: I'm sorry about you getting shot, what with you being home on your holidays and that. Do you know who did it?

Enter R.U.C. Special Branch Detective.

DET: Thank you, Constable. That'll be all for now. You can wait outside.

P/W smiles at Brid as she leaves. Detective draws up chair closer to bedside. Pause.

DET: Well, Miss Murphy. And what's your answer to the Constable's question?

BRID: I was hoping you could tell me, or haven't you checked up yet who's on duty in the Shoot to Kill Squad tonight?

DET: Miss Murphy. Brid. That's not a line of argument useful to either of us.

BRID: You can drop the patronizing tone, 'Inspector'. And I'd like to be addressed as Ms Murphy. But I'd prefer not to be addressed by you at all.

Detective gets up. Begins pacing to and fro.

DET: You reside in London, Miss Murphy — at 14 Kentish Town Avenue, London NW5. Is that correct?

BRID: Correct.

DET: And I understand you're home on holiday visiting your parents who live at 9 Milltown Park, Belfast BT11 9DG?

BRID: Correct.

DET: Where were you tonight, Miss Murphy?

BRID: Tonight?

DET: Yes. Tonight. Before you were picked up by the Ambulance Service and brought to this hospital?

BRID: I was out for a drink with my sisters.

DET: Their names?

BRID: Aine and Caitlin.

DET: Aine Murphy, also of 9 Milltown Park and Mrs Caitlin Doyle of 63 River Street.

BRID: Why the questions when you have it all on your computer?

DET: This drink. Where did you and your sisters have it?

BRID: In a bar.

DET: Which bar, Miss Murphy?

BRID: McBride's.

DET: The Republican club?

BRID: Is it? I wouldn't know, Inspector. I'm just home on holiday. Visitin'!

DET: How many drinks did you and your sisters have in McBride's?

BRID: Not enough.

DET: Did you speak to anyone in McBride's?

BRID: Yes.

BRID: The barman.

DET: Anyone else?

BRID: Yes.

DET: Who?

BRID: My sisters. Aine and Caitlin.

DET: Did you speak to anyone apart from the barman and your sisters?

BRID: No.

DET: No old friends? Acquaintances?

BRID: I've been away a long time, Inspector. Faces change.

DET: How *long* have you been away, Miss Murphy?

BRID: In London?

DET: Yes. In London.

BRID: Fourteen years.

DET: And what do you do there?

BRID: I'm a teacher.

BRID: You're not married, Miss Murphy?

BRID: No.

DET: Living with someone?

BRID: That's none of your business, Inspector.

DET: (*aside*) Touchy about being unmarried. . . Did you go to Queens University before going to London?

BRID: No.

DET: Where then?

BRID: Liverpool.

DET: Were you ever politically involved, Miss Murphy?

BRID: I seem to be at the moment with this interrogation.

DET: I meant student politics. Marches. Demonstrations. Here or in Liverpool?

BRID: What does it say on your computer, Inspector?

DET: At what time did you leave the McBride's club tonight?

BRID: Probably coming up to about half eleven.

DET: With your sisters?

BRID: No. They had left before me. Caitlin was concerned about her children and Aine said she'd walk back with her.

DET: Strange you didn't leave with them, Miss Murphy.

BRID: I hadn't finished my drink and you know what it's like, you hate leaving it.

DET: So you left McBride's at about 11.30. Alone?

BRID: Correct.

DET: And you set off. Alone. To walk home.

BRID: It's only a dander of about ten minutes from McBride's to my mother's.

DET: Describe what happened then.

BRID: It's in the statement I gave on arrival at the hospital.

DET: You heard a car behind you. Then a shot. And then you felt a pain in your arm. And you fainted.

BRID: Correct.

DET: Who rang for the ambulance, Miss Murphy?

BRID: I suppose somebody in the nearby houses must've heard the shooting. Maybe they saw a body lying by the kerb. I don't know, Inspector. Remember, I had fainted.

DET: Yes. So you said, Miss Murphy. So you said.

Enter policewoman.

P/W: Excuse me, Sir. There's a phone call for you.

Inspector and Brid exchange looks. Inspector leaves. Policewoman smiles at Brid. She sits. Pause.

P/W: He's a Catholic, you know.

BRID: Sorry? Who is?

P/W: The Inspector.

Brid laughs.

P/W: No. Seriously. I'm not joking you.

BRID: It's alright, Constable.I don't doubt your word.

P/W: Are you surprised?

BRID: That the Inspector is a Catholic? No, Constable, I'm not. In fact, if anything, he has the look of a priest about him.
Policewoman looks puzzled.
Pause.

P/W: Have you a man in London?

BRID: Yes, I have a man in London.

P/W: Patrick?

BRID: Sorry?

P/W: Your man in London. He's called Patrick?

BRID: No.

P/W: Oh? It's just that was the name you muttered in your sleep. Patrick.
Exchange of looks. Hold and fade to music.

SCENE 11

Murphy home. Tommy, Nora, Brid and Aine.

TOMMY: They're bastards. Fuckin' bastards!

NORA: Tommy?

TOMMY: Of course, since Stalker, they know they can get away with it. They know they can go blargin' all around them left right and bloody centre. Not that it's really any different from what they've always done since this abortion of a six-county State was set up. And then they have the bloody nerve to interrogate you in hospital and ask innocently who do you think did it when they know it was one of their own crowd. . .

BRID: But you don't know that, Daddy. . .

TOMMY: What d'you mean I don't know that? Who the hell else do you think shot you? You didn't shoot yourself did you? It was the R.U.C., the Army or the Prods.

BRID: Or it could've been some internecine feud. . .

TOMMY: Inter. . . what? Jesus, Brid, you've definitely been living in England for too long for you're sounding like you've been tainted with their bloody excuse making for shitting the bed. . .

NORA: Tommy, will you stop shouting at the girl. Brid is probably still in a state of shock and all you can do is sound off like an editorial from *The Republican News* and slabber about people living in England. Is it any wonder she does live in England when this kind of thing happens? It's a wonder more don't leave. I'm telling you now, if I was young enough I'd be on the plane with her back to London.

TOMMY: Well, it's never too late, Nora. If you want to go and live in England with her and her fancy Englishman, then you go right ahead.

AINE: That's enough, Father. Shut up!

TOMMY: Are you speaking to me, girl?

AINE: Yes. I'm speaking to you. For maybe I know more about what happened last night than you do.

TOMMY: Oh, you do, do you? Well, maybe you'll want to be joining your mother on that plane. Then youse can all go and play happy English families in London. Christ, don't tell me I've reared a family of Brit-lovers!

AINE: No, Father, you haven't. But you haven't reared a family of narrow, unthinking bigots either. What happened last night to Brid is appalling. Appalling things have been going on in this country for the last twenty years and nobody in this house has any illusions about the nature of the British Government's policy in Ireland. But some of us are not so blind as to see it only in the outmoded ranting slogans of over seventy years ago.

TOMMY: So, it's outmoded now to be Irish, is it? Christ, what's wrong with you bloody women? Do youse like suffering or what?

NORA: No, Tommy. We do not. But at this point in time you're the one who's making *us* suffer. There's no Brits or R.U.C. or Loyalists in this kitchen at the moment, but we're being treated as badly as if they were all hammering the livin' daylights out of us. Now, will you do what your daughter suggests and shut up. Just shut up, Tommy. Enough. Enough.

Nora close to tears, sits down, back to others. Tommy looks at Nora, then at Aine and Brid. He lifts jacket and leaves. Pause. Enter Caitlin.

CAITLIN: What the hell is going on in this house? I just met my Daddy in the street and he shouted 'and when are you leaving for England with the rest of them?' What's been going on? And what happened to you, Brid? Wrestling with that Pat O'Brien all night were you?

Mrs Murphy turns round. Looks at Caitlin. Then at Aine and Brid.

Hold. Blackout — sound and music.

SCENE | 12

Bedroom in Murphy home. Aine and Brid in bed.

BRID: You've been to Paris, haven't you, Aine?

AINE: Once. I acted as second jailer along with the head of French when we took a party of girls for a week. But I wouldn't call it 'having been to Paris'.

BRID: John and I were there last summer. It's the fourth trip we've made. We did all the usual things. Sat in cafés. Gazed at Van Gogh in the Jeu de Paume. Inhaled Gauloises. Browsed in bookshops. Strolled in the Luxembourg Gardens. Saw an arty film one wet afternoon which turned out to be French soft porn. Ate. Drank wine. But there was one afternoon we went to visit distant cousins of John's. They're actually cousins of his grandfather's. John's grandfather was Jewish.

AINE: I didn't know that. . .

BRID: Neither did John until recently. His father never talks about matters Jewish or anything like that. Anyway, we went to see these cousins. They live on the outskirts of Paris. They're both in their seventies. We had lunch together and it was all very pleasant. They're Roumanian. Jewish. They told us about their lives. And you know, Aine, it would have made you weep. They were in hiding during the war. They lived in a forest for over 12 months at the time of the Nazis. Then after the war, it was the time of Stalin and both of them were imprisoned for I can't remember exactly how long. And then eventually they were released. Finally in the early seventies, they were allowed to leave. They came to Paris. He had some friends there. And you know, Aine, sitting at that lunch table in their apartment on the outskirts of Paris, I felt like I was sitting beside the history of the 20th Century. And in a way I was. Those two old people were survivors. Survivors of Nazism. Survivors of Stalinism . . . they had suffered pain you and I can't even imagine . . . they had lived through the most barbaric of times and yet there they were, entertaining John and me to lunch in Paris. Asking us questions. Interested in our lives. Chatting of their plans to visit Israel. It was one of the most 'joyful' afternoons I've ever had. And as if this experience wasn't enough, John and I on the way back to the centre of Paris on the train were studying maps. A street map of Paris. Map of France. Map of Europe. And suddenly I looked — as if I'd never seen them before — on the map of Europe to the North West. The two islands of Britain and Ireland. Tiny, Insignificant. Cast off from the main land mass.

Surrounded by water. And I thought of what went on between them — these two minute islands. The hatred. The bigotry. The ignorance. The stupidity. The violence. The pain. The suffering. And I thought of the two old Jews I had just left. And I didn't know whether to weep with impotence and emptiness or cry out in rage and despair. And for a moment I didn't know whether I wanted to see those two pathetic islands sink into the Atlantic or clasp them warmly together and pull them towards Europe. . .

Pause.

AINE: Which did you decide, Brid?

Brid shrugs.
Pause.

BRID: I think I'll leave tomorrow.

Music. Fade.

SCENE 13

Murphy home.

NORA: What sort of a country has Ireland become that its young people feel the need always to leave? Even the priest this morning at Mass was talking of how Ireland's biggest export is its people. What's wrong with us at all that in a Catholic country we seem only to be known for murdering each other and emigrating?

TOMMY: We're known for other things, Nora.

NORA: What, Tommy? What? Breeding racehorses for the Queen Mother?

TOMMY: Look at the artists we've given to the world.

NORA: Aye. And it was into the world they had to go to be recognized, for their own gave them nothing but would feed off them after they were dead. Oh, we're great at claimin' them back after the world has informed us of their existence.

TOMMY: There's plenty who stay, Nora. Not all the young ones are leaving. There's those who've been fighting and dying for Ireland.

NORA: Yes, Tommy. We're awful good at funerals. Is that the alternative to leaving? Stay. Fight. And die. And then we'll drape your coffin with a tricolour. Cry for a while. Then forget you.

TOMMY: We don't forget them. Ireland has always honoured her dead.

NORA: Maybe, it's time she started honouring her living. We don't forget? I bet you can't name the ten dead hunger-strikers?

TOMMY: Bobby Sands, Francis Hughes, Mickey Devine. . .

Enter Pat O'Brien.

PAT: Tom McIlwee, Raymond McCreesh, Patsy O'Hara, Kieran Doherty, Joe O'Donnell, Martin Hurson, Kevin Lynch. . .

NORA: Who the hell are you? How did you get in here?

PAT: The back door was open, Mrs Murphy. . .

NORA: How do you know my name?

TOMMY: Do youse want to use the house to have a blarge at the Brits?

NORA: Christ, Tommy, have you taken leave of your senses?

PAT: No. Mrs Murphy. I just called to see Brid. Is she in?

NORA: And how do you know our Brid?

Enter Brid, from upstairs.

BRID: It's all right, Mother. Relax. This gentleman helped me the other night.

NORA: He did? So this is Patrick O'Brien?

TOMMY: See, Nora. Ireland's young. The finest. Well, we'll leave you, Comrade, to have a chat. Maybe you can find out why my daughter can't wait to leave her own hearth again. . .

NORA: Brid?

BRID: It's alright, Mother.

Tommy and Nora leave.
Silence.

BRID: I didn't expect to see you again so soon. Aren't you taking a risk calling here?

PAT: I'm not stopping long . . . I. . .

BRID: You don't seem to stop long anywhere. . .

PAT: I'm sorry I couldn't stay with you the other night . . . but . . . I saw the ambulance take you away so I figured . . . and I phoned the hospital later on.

BRID: Yes. The nurse told me an 'old flame' had rung to enquire how I was.

PAT: You're alright then?

BRID: I'm not dead.

Pause.

PAT: Did the. . .

BRID: Yes. They did. But don't worry, I didn't shop you. I said I was walking home on my own.

PAT: Did they believe you?

BRID: No. Would you? They wanted to know who 'phoned the ambulance. I said, somebody must've heard the shooting from the houses opposite and rung for one.

PAT: Is that all?

BRID: Apart from all the usual questions like what did I eat for breakfast and how many orgasms did I have last year?

Pat smiles.

PAT: Thanks, Brid. And I am sorry. . .

BRID: Who do you think it was?

PAT: Was?

BRID: Who shot at us?

Pat shrugs.

BRID: Was it an internal job?

PAT: What do you mean?

BRID: Oh, don't insult me, Pat O'Brien. I mean it has been known for one sort of Republican to shoot another kind of Republican, hasn't it?

PAT: Not recently, Brid. All that's over.

BRID: Strange though the way it happened, don't you think? Us, drinking in McBride's club. Who else would know your movements? And we hadn't left the club that long. . .

PAT: The Loyalists or the Brits don't have to study your form, Brid. You just have to be a Taig in a Taig district.

BRID: So, it wasn't necessarily you they were after. . .

PAT: What do you think?

BRID: I think, Pat O'Brien, Irish history isn't a nightmare from which we're trying to awaken. It's a living hell that consumes us every sleeping and waking hour. . .

  Silence.

PAT: When are you leaving?

BRID: Tonight. I'm taking the 6.30 shuttle back to London.

PAT: Do you have to go?

BRID: Why? Have you called round to see if the other night's offer is still on?

  Silence.

BRID: I'm sorry. That was out of line. I was out of line talkin' that way then as well.

  Pause.

PAT: Do you love him?

BRID: You mean how could I possibly love an Englishman?

PAT: No, Brid. I didn't mean that (*Pause*) Look, I better be going. . . (*Pat goes to door, turns*) He must be some character for a woman like you. . . Pity Ireland's so short of them. Watch your step, Brid. All the best.

  Pat steps forward. Kisses Brid on cheek. Exits.

BRID: All the best. Ireland.

  Blackout — music and sound.

British Airways shuttle aircraft. Brid and an Englishman, a fellow passenger. Upstage in shadow, Caitlin and Aine.

VOICE OF STEWARD: Good evening, ladies and gentlemen. On behalf of Captain Smith and his crew, welcome to our British Airways Supershuttle flight BA 125 Belfast to Heathrow, London. Our flying time this evening will be approximately fifty minutes. The safety equipment on board our aircraft. . .

BRID: 9 Milltown Park. West Belfast. A taxi sitting at the front door. Time to go. Leave. All the Best. Ireland. All the Best. Mother. Father. Standing at the front door. Father. Hands in pockets. Falsely nonchalant. The hard man of Andytown politics. Does he know he's posing? Or has the pose become the man? Mother. Dabbing her eyes with a handkerchief. She looks old. Sad. How many more years before we say goodbye for the last . . . time?

ENGLISHMAN: Been ski-ing on the Mountains of Mourne have you? (*Referring to Brid's arm in sling*) Actually, my wife's people are from Northern Ireland. That's going back a bit, though.

BRID: Caitlin. My little sister. The baby. Strange to think of her as a wife and mother. Doesn't seem right somehow. She's not old enough to be reproducing the tribe. Will anything ever change?

CAITLIN: Maybe the next time I see you, Brid, you'll have produced a cousin for my boys. Certainly, by then, I'll have had this one (*puts stomach*). And who knows, maybe another, if the juices and hormones keep bubbling. Do you think I should keep trying until I get a girl? Mind you, that way I could just end up with a Gaelic football team. That would please my Da . . . the Murphy Gaelic Athletic Association! Enjoy yourself, Brid.

ENGLISHMAN: Yes. My wife's family sold up and got out in the last troubles. In the 1920's, wasn't it? You'll know the history better than me.

BRID: Aine. My big sister. Beautiful. Sad. A look of defeat. Resignation settling into the first wrinkles on her attractive face.

AINE: I'll never leave now, Brid. Not now. It's too late. You need to go, if you're going, when you're still young enough to believe in people. And change. Ireland's stuck with me. And I'm stuck with Ireland. Maybe I'll go over to visit you and John in the summer time. Yiz can 'show me the sights'. Look after yourself, Brid. Write to me. I love you, sister.

ENGLISHMAN: Of course I know we English haven't exactly played fair in the history of Ireland as my wife keeps reminding me. But Mrs Thatcher, I think, is making more of an effort to help. I mean, the Anglo-Irish Agreement has got to be a good thing, don't you think?

Brid gives Englishman a withering look. Blackout and sound.
Voice of steward.
Heathrow Airport. Brid carrying suitcase. Man and woman approach Brid.

MAN: Miss Brid Murphy?

BRID: *Brid* Murphy! Yes.

MAN: Police. (*shows I.D.*) Miss Murphy, we're arresting you under the Prevention of Terrorism Act. Would you come this way, please?

Hold, then slow fade.

Other plays published by Marion Boyars Publishers